DOLL BONES

DOLL BONES

Holly Black

With illustrations by Eliza Wheeler

Margaret K. McElderry Books
New York London Toronto Sydney New Delhi

MARGARET K. McELDERRY BOOKS

An imprint of Simon & Schuster Children's Publishing Division

1230 Avenue of the Americas, New York, New York 10020

This book is a work of fiction. Any references to historical events, real people, or real places are used fictitiously. Other names, characters, places, and events are products of the author's imagination, and any resemblance to actual events or places or persons, living or dead, is entirely coincidental.

Text copyright © 2013 by Holly Black

Illustrations copyright © 2013 by Simon & Schuster, Inc.

All rights reserved, including the right of reproduction in whole or in part in any form.

MARGARET K. McELDERRY BOOKS is a trademark of Simon & Schuster, Inc.

For information about special discounts for bulk purchases, please contact Simon & Schuster Special Sales at 1-866-506-1949 or business@simonandschuster.com.

The Simon & Schuster Speakers Bureau can bring authors to your live event. For more information or to book an event, contact the Simon & Schuster Speakers Bureau at 1-866-248-3049 or visit our website at www.simonspeakers.com.

Also available in a Margaret K. McElderry Books hardcover edition

Book design by Sonia Chaghatzbanian

The text for this book is set in Adobe Caslon Pro.

The illustrations for this book are rendered in pencil.

Manufactured in the United States of America

1018 OFF

First Margaret K. McElderry Books paperback edition April 2015

8 10 9

The Library of Congress has cataloged the hardcover edition as follows:

Black, Holly.

Doll bones / Holly Black.—1st ed.

p. cm.

Summary: Zach, Alice, and Poppy, friends from a Pennsylvania middle school who have long enjoyed acting out imaginary adventures with dolls and action figures, embark on a real-life quest to Ohio to bury a doll made from the ashes of a dead girl.

ISBN 978-1-4169-6398-1 (hardcover)

ISBN 978-1-4424-7487-1 (eBook)

[1. Adventure and adventurers—Fiction. 2. Friendship—Fiction. 3. Dolls—Fiction. 4. Ghosts—Fiction. 5. Family problems—Fiction.] I. Title.

PZ7.B52878Dol 2013

[Fic]—dc23

ISBN 978-1-4169-6399-8 (pbk)

2012018299

For Katherine Rudden,
who played the game with
me long after we were old
enough to stop

❧ CHAPTER ONE ❧

POPPY SET DOWN ONE OF THE MERMAID DOLLS CLOSE
to the stretch of asphalt road that represented the Blackest
Sea. They were old—bought from Goodwill—with big
shiny heads, different-colored tails, and frizzy hair.

Zachary Barlow could almost imagine their fins
lashing back and forth as they waited for the boat to get
closer, their silly plastic smiles hiding their lethal inten-
tions. They'd crash the ship against the shallows if they
could, lure the crew into the sea, and eat the pirates with
their jagged teeth.

Zachary rummaged through his bag of action figures. He pulled out the pirate with the two cutlasses and
placed him gently at the center of the boat-shaped paper
they'd weighed down with driveway gravel. Without

gravel, the *Neptune's Pearl* was likely to blow away in the early autumn wind. He could almost believe he wasn't on the scrubby lawn in front of Poppy's ramshackle house with the sagging siding, but aboard a real ship, with salt spray stinging his face, on his way to adventure.

"We're going to have to lash ourselves to the mast," Zach said, as William the Blade, captain of the *Neptune's Pearl*. Zach had a different way of speaking for each of his figures. He wasn't sure that anyone but him could tell his voices apart, but he felt different when he talked in them.

Alice's braids spilled in front of her amber eyes as she moved a G.I. Joe Lady Jaye figure closer to the center of the boat. Lady Jaye was a thief who'd begun traveling with William the Blade after she'd been unsuccessful in picking his pocket. She was loud and wild, almost nothing like Alice, who chafed under the thumb of her overprotective grandmother, but did it quietly.

"You think the Duke's guards will be waiting for us in Silverfall?" Alice made Lady Jaye ask.

"He might catch us," said Zach, grinning at her. "But he'll never hold us. Nothing will. We're on a mission for the Great Queen and we won't be stopped." He hadn't expected to say those words until they came out of his mouth, but they felt right. They felt like William's true thoughts.

That was why Zach loved playing: those moments where it seemed like he was accessing some other world, one that felt real as anything. It was something he never wanted to give up. He'd rather go on playing like this forever, no matter how old they got, although he didn't see how that was possible. It was already hard sometimes.

Poppy tucked windblown strands of red hair behind her ears and regarded Zach and Alice very seriously. She was tiny and fierce, with freckles thick enough to remind Zach of the stars at night. She liked nothing better than being in charge of the story and had a sense of how to make a moment dramatic. That was why she was the best at playing villains.

"You can knot ropes to keep you safe, but no boat can pass through these waters unless a sacrifice is given to the deep," Poppy made one of the mermaids say. "Willingly or unwillingly. If one of your crew doesn't leap into the sea, the sea will choose her own sacrifice. That's the mermaid's curse."

Alice and Zach exchanged a look. Were the mermaids telling the truth? Really, Poppy wasn't supposed to make up rules like that—ones that no one else had agreed to—but Zach objected only when he didn't like them. A curse seemed like it could be fun.

"We'll all go down together before we lose a single member of this crew," he fake-shouted in William's voice. "We're on a mission for the Great Queen, and we fear her curse more than yours."

"But just then," said Poppy ominously, moving one of the mermaids to the edge of the ship, "webbed fingers grab Lady Jaye's ankle, and the mermaid pulls her over the side of the boat. She's gone."

"You can't do that!" Alice said. "I was lashed to the mast."

"You didn't specify that you were," Poppy told her. "William suggested it, but you didn't say whether or not you did it."

Alice groaned, as though Poppy was being especially annoying. Which she kind of was. "Well, Lady Jaye was in the *middle of the boat*. Even if she wasn't lashed, a mermaid couldn't get to her without crawling on board."

"If Lady Jaye gets pulled over the side, I'm going after her," Zach said, plunging William into the gravel water. "I meant it when I said no one gets left behind."

"I didn't get pulled over the side," Alice insisted.

As they continued arguing two of Poppy's brothers

walked out of the house, letting the screen door slam behind them. They looked over and started to snicker. The older of the two, Tom, pointed directly at Zach and said something under his breath. His younger brother laughed.

Zach felt his face heat. He didn't think they knew anyone at his middle school, but still. If any of his teammates found out that, at twelve, he was still playing with action figures, basketball would become a lot less fun. School could get bad too.

"Ignore them," Poppy declared loudly. "They're jerks."

"All we were going to say is that Alice's grandma called," Tom said, his face a parody of hangdog innocence. He and Nate had the same tomato-red hair as their sister, but they weren't much like her in any other way that Zach could see. They, along with their eldest sister, were always in trouble—fighting, cutting school, smoking, and other stuff. The Bell kids were considered hoodlums in town and, Poppy aside, they seemed intent on doing what they could to uphold that reputation. "Old lady Magnaye says that you need to be home before dark and for us to be sure to tell you not to forget or make excuses. She seems rough, Alice." The words were supposed to be nice, but you could tell from the sickly sweet way Tom talked that he wasn't being nice at all.

Alice stood up and brushed off her skirt. The orange glow of the setting sun bronzed her skin and turned her glossy box braids metallic. Her eyes narrowed. Her expression wavered between flustered and angry. Boys had been hassling her ever since she'd hit ten, gotten curves, and started looking a lot older than she was. Zach hated the way Tom talked to her, like he was making fun of her without really saying anything bad, but he never knew what to say to stop it either.

"Leave off," Zach told them.

The Bell boys laughed. Tom mimicked Zach, making his voice high-pitched. "*Leave off.* Don't talk to my girlfriend."

"Yeah, *leave off*," Nate squeaked. "Or I'll beat you up with my doll."

Alice started toward the Bell house, head down.

Great, Zach thought. As usual, he'd made it worse.

"Don't go yet," Poppy called to Alice, ignoring her brothers. "Call home and just see if you can spend the night."

"I better not," Alice said. "I've just got to get my backpack from inside."

"Wait up," Zach said, grabbing Lady Jaye. He

headed for the screen door and got there just as it shut in his face. "You forgot—"

The inside of Poppy's house was always a mess. Discarded clothes, half-empty cups, and sports equipment covered most surfaces. Her parents seemed to have given up on the house around the same time they gave up on trying to enforce any rules about dinners and bedtimes and fighting—around Poppy's eighth birthday, when one of her brothers threw her cake with its still-lit birthday candles at her older sister. Now there were no more birthday parties. There weren't even family meals, just boxes of macaroni and cheese, cans of ravioli, and tins of sardines in the pantry so that the kids could feed themselves long before their parents came home from work and fell, exhausted, into their bed.

Zach felt envious every time he thought of that kind of freedom, and Alice loved it even more than he did. She spent as many nights there as her grandmother allowed. Poppy's parents didn't seem to notice, which worked out pretty perfectly.

He opened the screen door and went inside.

Alice was standing in front of the dusty, old, locked display cabinet in the corner of the Bell living room, peering in at all the things Poppy's mother had forbidden Poppy, on pain of death and possible dismemberment, from touching. That was where the doll they called the Great Queen of all their kingdoms was trapped, next to a blown-glass vase from Savers that had turned out to be vintage something-or-other. The Queen had been picked up by Poppy's mother at a tag sale, and she insisted that one day she was going to go on *Antiques Roadshow*, sell it, and move them all to Tahiti.

The Queen was a bone china doll of a child with straw-gold curls and paper-white skin. Her eyes were closed, lashes a flaxen fringe against her cheek. She wore a long gown, the thin fabric dotted with something black that might be mold. Zach couldn't remember when exactly they'd decided that she was the Great Queen, only that they'd all felt like she was watching them, even though her eyes were closed, and that Poppy's sister had been terrified of her.

Apparently, one time, Poppy had woken in the middle of the night and found her sister—with whom she shared a room—sitting upright in bed. "If she gets out of the case, she'll come for us," her sister had said, blank-faced, before slumping back down on her pillow. No amount of calling to the other side of the room had seemed to stir her. Poppy had tossed and

turned, unable to sleep for the rest of the night. But in the morning, her sister had told her that she didn't remember saying anything, that it must have been a nightmare, and that their mother really needed to get rid of that doll.

After that, to avoid being totally terrified, Zach, Poppy, and Alice had added the doll to their game.

According to the legend they'd created, the Queen ruled over everything from her beautiful glass tower. She had the power to put her mark on anyone who disobeyed her commands. When that happened, nothing would go right for them until they regained her favor. They'd be convicted of crimes they didn't commit. Their friends and family would sicken and die. Ships would sink, and storms would strike. The one thing the Queen couldn't do, though, was escape.

"You okay?" Zach asked Alice. She seemed transfixed by the case, staring into it as though she could see something Zach couldn't.

Finally Alice turned around, her eyes shining. "My grandmother wants to know where I am every second. She wants to pick out my clothes for me and complains about my braids all the time. I just am so over it. And I don't know if she's going to let me be in the play this year, even though I got a good part. She can't see so well after dark, and she doesn't want to drive me home. I'm just so tired of all her rules, and it's like the older I get, the worse she gets."

Zach had heard most of that before, but usually Alice just sounded resigned to it. "What about your aunt? Could you ask her to pick you up after rehearsals?"

Alice snorted. "She's never forgiven Aunt Linda for trying to get custody of me way back when. Brings it up at every holiday. It's made her superparanoid."

Mrs. Magnaye grew up in the Philippines and was fond of telling anyone who would listen how different things were over there. According to her, Filipino teenagers worked hard, never talked back, and didn't draw on their hands with ink pens or want to be actresses, like Alice did. They didn't get as tall as Alice was getting either.

"*Made* her superparanoid?" Zach asked.

Alice laughed. "Yeah, okay. Made her extra-superparanoid."

"Hey." Poppy came into the living room from outside, holding the rest of their figures. "Are you *sure* you can't stay over, Alice?"

Alice shook her head, plucked Lady Jaye out of Zach's hand, and went down the hallway to Poppy's room. "I was just getting my stuff."

Poppy turned impatiently to Zach for an explanation. She never liked it when she wasn't part of a conversation and hated the idea that her friends had kept any secrets from her, even stupid ones.

"Her grandmother," he said, with a shrug. "You know."

Poppy sighed and looked at the cabinet. After a moment, she spoke. "If you finish this quest, the Queen will probably lift the curse on William. He could go home and finally solve the mystery of where he came from."

"Or maybe she'll just make him do another quest." He thought about it a moment and grinned. "Maybe she wants him to get skilled enough with a sword to break her out of that cabinet."

"Don't even think about it," Poppy said, only half joking. "Come on."

They walked down the hall to Poppy's room just as Alice came out, backpack over one shoulder.

"See you tomorrow," she said as she slipped past them. She didn't look happy, but Zach thought she might just be upset that she was leaving early and that they were going to be hanging out without her. He and Poppy didn't *usually* play the game when Alice wasn't there. But lately Alice seemed to be more bothered by he and Poppy spending time alone together, which he didn't understand.

Zach walked into Poppy's room and flopped down on her orange shag rug. Poppy used to share the room with her older sister, and piles of her sister's outgrown clothes still remained spread out in drifts, along with a collection of used makeup and notebooks covered in stickers and scrawled with lyrics. A jumble of her sister's old Barbies were on top of a bookshelf, waiting for Poppy to try to fix their melted arms and chopped hair. The bookshelves were overflowing with fantasy paperbacks and overdue library books, some of them on Greek myths, some on mermaids, and a few on local hauntings. The walls were covered in posters— *Doctor Who*, a cat in a bowler hat, and a giant map of Narnia. Zach thought about drawing a map of their kingdoms—one with the oceans and the islands and everything—and wondered where he could get a big enough piece of paper.

"Do you think that William likes Lady Jaye?" Poppy asked, settling herself cross-legged on her bed, the pale pink of one knee visible through the rip in her hand-me-down jeans. "Like *like* likes?"

He sat up. "What?"

"William and Lady Jaye," she said. "They've been

traveling together awhile, right? I mean, he must like her some."

"Sure he likes her," Zach said, frowning. He pulled his beat-up army surplus duffel bag toward him and stuffed William inside.

"But, I mean, would he *marry* her?" Poppy asked.

Zach hesitated. He was used to being asked how characters felt, and it was a simple question. But there was something in Poppy's voice that made him think there was a meaning behind it that was less simple. "He's a *pirate*. Pirates don't get married. But, I mean—if he wasn't a pirate and she wasn't a crazy kleptomaniacal thief, then I guess he might."

Poppy sighed as though that was the worst answer ever given by anyone, but she dropped it. They talked about other things, like how Zach couldn't play the next day because of basketball practice, whether or not aliens would ever land, and if they did, whether they would be peaceful or not (they both thought not), and which one of them would be more useful in a zombie uprising (a draw, since Zach's longer legs would be better for getting away, and Poppy's small size was a hiding advantage).

On the way out, Zach paused in the living room to look at the Queen again. Her pale face was shadowed, but it seemed to him that though her eyes were closed, they weren't quite as closed as they had been before. While he stared at her, trying to figure out if he was imagining things, her lashes fluttered once, as if stirred by an impossible breeze.

Or as if she was a sleeper on the verge of awakening.

⊰◦ CHAPTER TWO ◦⊱

ZACHARY WAS ABOUT TO LEAVE FOR SCHOOL WHEN his father limped in from work. He stank of grease and favored his left foot. The restaurant he worked at closed around three in the morning, but checking the stock and reorders and getting a meal with the rest of the crew meant he came home much later than closing time most days.

"Bad blisters," Dad grunted, by way of explanation for the limping. His dad was a big guy with a mess of short curly hair the same burnt-toast color as Zach's, the same beach-glass blue eyes, and a nose that had been broken twice. "And then, like an idiot, I splashed oil on myself. But we were slammed, so that's something."

Slammed was good. Slammed meant that people

were eating at the restaurant, and that meant Zach's dad wasn't going to lose this job.

Mom got out a mug, poured coffee into it wordlessly, and set it down on the table. Zach grabbed his backpack, heading for the door. He felt bad, but it sometimes still surprised him to see his father in the house. His dad had moved out three years ago and moved back in three months ago. Zach couldn't get used to him being around.

"Tear up that court today," his dad said, tousling Zach's hair as though he was a little kid.

His father loved that Zach was on the basketball team. Sometimes that seemed as if it was the only thing about Zach he liked. He didn't like that Zach played with girls after school instead of shooting hoops with the older kids a couple of blocks over. He didn't like that Zach daydreamed all the time. And sometimes it seemed to Zach that his father didn't even like that Zach had gotten really good at basketball, since it meant that he couldn't scold Zach about how all that other stuff was getting in the way of his performance on the court.

Mostly, Zach didn't care what his dad thought. Every time his dad gave him a disapproving look or asked a question that was supposed to make him defensive,

Zach would pretend not to notice. Zach and his mom had been fine before his father moved back in, and they'd be fine when he left again, too.

With a sigh, Zach started toward school. Usually, he met up with some of the other walkers, but today the only other kid he saw walking was Kevin Lord. Kevin told Zach a long story about seeing deer when he was riding his dirt bike through the woods and ate a toaster pastry thing, raw, right out of the wrapping.

Zach got to Mr. Lockwood's class just after the buses. Alex Rios leaned back in his chair to bring his fist down on top of Zach's. Then they both slapped their hands together and dragged them until they were hooked by the ends of their fingers. It was a handshake taught to everyone on the basketball team, and every time that Zach did it, he felt the warm buzz of belonging.

"You think we're going to win against Edison next Sunday?" Alex asked in a way that wasn't really asking. It was part of the ritual, like the handshake.

"We're going to wreck them," said Zach, "so long as you keep passing me the ball."

Alex snorted, and then Mr. Lockwood started to take attendance, so they turned toward the SMART board. Zach tried to stop smiling and appear to be paying attention.

After lunch Poppy pressed a triangle-shaped note into his hand as she passed him in the hall. He didn't need to unfold it to know what it was. *Questions.* He couldn't remember which one of them had come up with the idea, or when, but Questions existed as a strange private thing outside the game. He and Poppy and Alice had to answer *any* in-game question they were asked, on paper, but the answers were only for the questioner. Characters didn't get to know.

They passed notes back and forth, especially if one of them was about to get grounded or before someone went on a trip. He always felt a flush of excitement— and a little bit of dread—when he got a folded-up paper. It was a part of the game that felt particularly risky. If a teacher got ahold of the note or Alex saw it—just thinking about the possibility made the back of Zach's neck burn with embarrassment.

He unfolded the sheet carefully, smoothing it against the pages of his textbook as Mr. Lockwood started his history lecture.

If the curse was lifted, would William really give up being a pirate? If he did, would he miss it?

Who does he think his father is?

Does he think that Lady Jaye likes him?

Does William ever have nightmares?

He started to scribble. He liked the way the story unfolded as he wrote, liked the way the answers just came to him sometimes, out of the blue, like they were true things just waiting to be discovered by him.

Sometimes William has dreams about being buried alive. He dreams that he's woken up and everything is black. He only knows where he is because he feels a heavy pressure on his chest and it's hard to get enough of a breath to scream. Usually, it's the trying to scream that wakes him. He finds himself swinging in a hammock in his quarters, in a cold sweat, his green parrot peering at him suspiciously with her single black eye. And he tells himself that when he's buried, he's going to be buried at sea.

Even after he folded the questions back into the shape of a football and tucked it into the front pocket of his backpack, the feeling of the story being close stayed with him. Zach doodled pictures in the margins of his notebook, drawings of cutlasses and blast rifles and crowns next to geometry homework and facts about the Battle of Antietam.

That past summer, the mysterious thing that had stretched other boys like taffy had started to happen to Zach. He'd always been tall, but now he'd almost reached his father's height, with hands so big that catching a basketball was a lot easier and legs so long that he could jump nearly high enough to touch the net. The year before, he'd hung back on the court, but now he was thundering down it.

Everyone at school looked at him differently all of a sudden. The guys were wanting to hang out more, slapping him on the back, and laughing louder at his jokes. And the girls had just gotten weird.

Even Alice acted strange around him sometimes. When she was with her school friends, instead of her talking to him like she usually did, the whole bunch of them giggled uncomfortably. That very afternoon, after practice, he passed by Alice and a few girls from the theater crew. They fled in a fit of shrieking laughter before he could ask Alice what had been so funny or whether she wanted to walk home with him.

So he walked home by himself, feeling a little bit

lonely as he made his way through the early autumn evening, kicking the carpet of fallen leaves. He didn't know how else to make things go back to normal. It wasn't like he could *shrink* himself back into being the same as before.

An eerie wind sang through the untrimmed trees in front of Mr. Thompson's old house at the end of the block. It sounded like someone shrieking from a long way off, but getting closer with every second. Zach sped up his pace, walking faster and faster, feeling foolish as he did it. He felt the tickle of the hairs on the back of his neck, as though whatever was coming was right behind him, as though he could feel its breath.

Suddenly he felt overwhelmed by a wash of terror. It was all-consuming and, despite feeling silly, he ran, racing across his lawn to the small brick house where he lived. He hit the front door, his palms slamming against it, and had to stumble back to jerk it open.

The kitchen smelled like spaghetti sauce and frying sausages, a warm, safe smell that drove away all thoughts of the night and the eerie wind.

His mother stuck her head out of the kitchen. She was wearing sweatpants, and her long brown hair was pulled back in a bunch of clips. She looked tired. "Dinner's almost ready. Why don't you start on your homework, and I'll call you when it's time to eat."

"Okay," Zach said. As he walked through the living room his dad was coming down the stairs. He clapped his hand heavily on Zach's shoulder.

"You're growing up," he said, which seemed to be one of those weird things adults would say sometimes, stuff that was really obvious and to which there was no reply.

Since his dad had come back, he'd been really fond of saying that kind of thing.

"I guess." Zach shrugged off his dad's grip and went up to his room.

He dumped his backpack out on the bed and sprawled on his stomach, reaching for his social studies book. He read the chapter he was supposed to and then started on punctuation, toeing off his sneakers. It was hard to concentrate. His stomach gurgled with hunger, and the smell of dinner made waiting to eat even harder. He was tired from practice, and the last thing he wanted to do was more schoolwork. He wanted to sit in front of the television and watch the show about ghost-hunters or the one with the thief who worked for the government. Ideally, he'd be watching them from the couch, with a huge plate of spaghetti and sausage on his lap.

Mom probably wasn't going to go for that, though. Ever since Dad was back, whenever he wasn't working, she was all about the family sitting together at the table without phones or games or books. She kept quoting something she'd read in a magazine—some kind of study that having dinner together was supposed to make Zach a happier adult and make her lose weight. Why they did it only when Dad was at home, if it was so important, Zach wasn't sure.

As all of this went through Zach's mind, something struck him as odd. That morning when he'd left for school, William the Blade had been sitting on the edge of his desk along with a bunch of the other action figures who were the semi-expendable crew for the *Neptune's Pearl*. But now none of them were there.

He glanced around the room. It wasn't very clean, even though every Sunday his mother made him "straighten it up a little." His dirty laundry was piled around his hamper more than in it. His bookshelf was stuffed with books on pirates, adventure novels, and textbooks that spilled onto the floor. His desk was crowded with magazines, his computer, LEGO pieces, and models of ships. But he knew the pattern of his mess. He knew where his guys should have been and where they were not.

He got up clumsily, half sliding off his mattress. Then he bent down to look under the bed. Their black cat, named "The Party," would sometimes sneak into his room and knock things over. As Zach squatted on the rug, though, he didn't see William the Blade anywhere on the floor.

He started to get anxious. William was his best character—the one he'd played the longest and the one that was still at the center of almost every one of his stories. Two weeks ago Poppy had introduced a fortune-teller who told William that she knew who his father was—and suddenly, while hunting down his past and trying to get the Queen's curse removed, William had become more fun to play than ever.

Poppy was always doing that—improvising, jumping into the gaps in a story, creating something new and interesting and a little scary. Sometimes it annoyed him—William's story was whatever Zach said it was, right?—but most of the time it was worth just giving in and trusting her.

It was important for William not to be missing. Because if William *was* missing, then there was no rest of the story, no more crazy ideas, no payoff, no ending, no more.

Maybe, he thought, maybe he was making a mistake. Maybe he'd misremembered where he'd left the figures. Maybe William and the others were with the rest of his toys. He walked over to where his duffel of action figures should have been, just inside his closet. But the bag wasn't there either.

He felt odd. Like something was pressing on his chest.

He stared at the spot, waiting for his brain to supply some explanation. Panic bloomed in him. He was sure the duffel had been resting on the floor that morning when he'd stumbled over it to get a T-shirt off a hanger.

But maybe he'd left it over at Poppy's house? Except that he *remembered* seeing it the night before. And he wouldn't have left it anywhere unless there was a reason— unless they were in the middle of an elaborate battle where everything had to stay exactly where it was. Which they were not.

He looked around helplessly.

"Mom!" Zach shouted, walking to the door of his room and flinging it open, stalking out into the hall. "Mom! What did you do with my stuff? Did you take my bag?"

"Zachary?" she called up from downstairs. "That's the second time you've slammed—"

He ran down the steps, cutting her off in mid-scold. "Where's my bag? The action figures. The models and cars. All of them. They're not upstairs."

"I didn't take anything out of your room. I bet it's underneath one of the Kilimanjaro-size piles of laundry up there." She smiled as she got down a stack of plates, but he didn't smile back. "Clean your room and I bet the bag turns up."

"No, Mom, they're *gone*." Zachary glanced over at his father and was surprised to see the expression on his dad's face—an expression he wasn't sure how to interpret.

She followed Zach's gaze, turning to Zach's father, her voice very quiet. "Liam?"

"He's twelve years old, playing with a bunch of crap," he said, getting up from the couch and raising his hands in a placating way. "He's got to grow up. It was time he got rid of them. He should be concentrating on friends, listening to music, goofing off. Zach, trust me, you won't miss them."

"Where are they?" Zach asked, a dangerous edge to his voice.

"Forget it, they're gone," his father said. "There's no point in throwing a tantrum."

"Those figures were *mine*!" Zach was so angry he could barely think. His voice shook with anger. "They were mine."

"Someone's got to get you ready for the real world,"

said his father, his face flushing red. "Be mad all you want, but it's done. Done. Do you understand me? It's time you grew up. End of discussion."

"Liam, what were you thinking?" Zach's mother demanded. "You can't just go making decisions without talking—"

"Where are they?" Zach snarled. He had never talked to his father this way, never talked to any adult this way. "What did you do with them?"

"Oh, don't be so dramatic," his dad said.

"Liam!" His mother's voice was cautioning.

"GIVE THEM BACK!" Zach shouted. He was out of control and he didn't care.

His father stopped for a moment, his expression suddenly uncertain. "I threw them out. I'm sorry. I didn't think you'd be this upset. They're just plastic—"

"In the garbage?" Zachary rushed out the door and down the steps. Two big dented metal trash cans were at the end of the lawn, resting on the curb. He pulled off the lid of one with numb fingers and threw it against the road with a *clang*.

Please, he thought. *Pleasepleaseplease.*

But the inside of the can was empty. The trash truck had already come and gone.

It felt like a punch to the gut. William the Blade

and Max Hunter and all the others were dead. Without them, all their stories would be dead too. He wiped his face against the sleeve of his shirt.

Then he turned back to the house. His father was silhouetted in the doorway.

"Hey, I'm sorry," he said.

"Don't bother trying to be my father anymore," Zach said, walking up the front steps and past him. "It's too late for that. It was too late years ago."

"Zachary," his mother said, her hand reaching out to touch his shoulder, but he walked past her.

His father just stared at him, his face stricken.

In his room, Zachary looked up at the ceiling, trying to quiet the feelings inside him. He didn't finish his homework. He didn't eat dinner, even though his mother brought up a plate and set it down on his desk. He didn't change out of his clothes into his pajamas. He didn't cry.

Zachary tossed and turned, concentrating on the shadows moving across the ceiling and on the anger that seemed to grow instead of lessen. He was angry. At his father, for destroying the game. At his mother, for letting his father back into their lives. At Poppy and Alice, who hadn't lost anything. And at himself, for acting like a little kid, just like his dad had said, and for caring about William the Blade and a bunch of plastic toys as though they were real people.

And that anger curdled inside his belly and crawled up his throat until it felt like it might choke him. Until he was sure that there was no way he could ever tell anyone what had happened without all of his anger spilling out and engulfing everything.

And the only way not to tell anyone was to end the game.

❦ CHAPTER THREE ❧

THE NEXT MORNING, ZACH PUSHED HIS LIMP CEREAL around in a bowl of milk as his mom poured herself a second cup of coffee. Light filtered in through the dirty windowpane to make the scarred wood on the kitchen table show the pale water marks from wet mugs and the greenish smudge where Zach had once drawn a spaceship in permanent marker. He traced the faint outline of it with a finger.

"Your father called the trash company last night," his mother said.

Zach blinked and looked up at her.

She took another sip of coffee. "He called the dump, too. Asked them if there was any way to get your toys back. He even offered to drive over there and look for them himself—but there was no way. I'm sorry. I know that he did a stupid thing, but he honestly tried to fix it, sweetheart."

Zach felt weirdly numb, as though everything that happened was on a slight delay. He knew what she was saying was supposed to be important, but somehow he couldn't make it matter. He felt tired, too, as though he hadn't slept at all, even though he'd actually slept so deeply that the ringing of his alarm had seemed to bring him up from the bottom of something deep and dark. He'd had to fight through his dreams to wake.

"Okay," he said, because there was nothing else to say.

"Tonight we're going to sit down and have a family discussion. Your dad was brought up by a very strict man and, as much as he hates it, he acts like his father sometimes. It's what he knows, honey."

Zach shrugged and put a scoop of soggy cereal in his mouth to keep from telling her that he'd rather be hung upside down by his toes over a blazing fire than talk to his father. Still chewing, he grabbed his backpack and started for school.

"We can discuss more later," his mother said with false cheer, moments before he slammed his way out the door.

The cold air felt like a slap in the face. He was relieved not to see Poppy and Alice on the sidewalk. They all lived close enough that sometimes they ran into each other on the way to school, and they usually walked home together. But this morning he hurried along the side of the street, glad to be alone. He kept his head down as he stalked along, kicking rocks and chunks of loose asphalt into the road. When he saw the school building in the distance, he wondered what would happen if he just kept going, the same way his father had left them three years ago. If he just kept walking until he came to a new place where no one knew him, lied about his age, and got a job delivering newspapers or something . . .

Well, he didn't know quite what he would do after that.

By the time he made up his mind to go to school, he was late. Mr. Lockwood glowered at him as he slunk into class just after the bell. He sat at his desk and drew nothing in the margins of his notebook. If a story idea came to him, he concentrated on something else until it went away.

At lunch his sandwich tasted like cardboard. He threw out his apple.

After school he told the coach he was too sick to go

to practice, but really, it was just that he didn't want to. He didn't much want to do anything.

He started walking home, thinking he could sit in front of the television until Mom got home from work, then tell her the same thing he told the coach. A few minutes later Alice caught up with him, the slap of her shoes on the pavement heralding her approach. He felt like an idiot for taking the same old route and not expecting to see any of his friends.

"Zach?" Alice asked, out of breath from running. She was wearing a blue T-shirt with a creature on it that appeared to be half brontosaurus, half kitten. Her braids were pulled back into a headband, and little feather earrings hung from her ears.

He had no idea what to say to her. He wanted to ask her about the day before when she was giggling with her friends—he wanted to know why she hadn't talked to him. But that seemed forever ago, and so much had happened since. He almost didn't feel like the same person.

A kid named Leo waved to them, walking in their direction. He had big glasses and was always saying crazy things. He was like a random generator of weirdness. "Hey," he said. "Poppy wanted me to tell you to walk slow. She's getting a book from the librarian."

"Oh," Zach said, feeling doomed. He knew what would happen next. One by one the mass of kids who walked home together would gather and then peel away into clumps headed in different directions, until it was just Poppy and Alice and him. Then one of them would ask, "Want to play?" like always. And he would have to say *something*.

"You okay?" Alice asked.

"Yeah," said Leo. "You don't look so good, Zach. Somebody walk over your grave?"

He blinked a couple of times. At least Leo was acting like his normal crazy self. That was one thing that wasn't going to change. *"What?"*

"That's what my grandpa always said. You never heard that?"

"No," Zach said. His foot sent a few leaves spiraling up into the air. Talking about graves made him think about walking home the night before, when he'd thought he heard the wind howling at his heels. He shivered. "So my grave is going to be in front of Thomas Peebles Middle School? That's so lame."

"It doesn't mean that you're going to be buried *here*." Alice rolled her eyes. "It's a saying. It means some*where* some*one* is stepping on the place where you're going to be buried."

"So it could be any old place?" Zach asked, shaking his head. "How does that help to know?"

"It's not supposed to help," Leo said. "It's just supposed to be true."

"What are you guys *talking* about?" Poppy asked, bounding up to them. She had on a black sweater and was bouncing on her blue Chucks, one of the pink laces untied and dragging muddily behind her. Her hair was in coppery pigtails, and her eyeliner looked smudged on one eye, like maybe she'd forgotten it was there and rubbed over it.

"Nothing," Zach said with a shrug.

Poppy looked over at Alice and raised her eyebrows. "Nothing like *nothing* or nothing like *something*?"

Alice shook her head and smiled, but then turned her smile down at the pavement, like she was embarrassed. Zach had no idea what was going on. He wondered if it had to do with yesterday and the giggling, but couldn't think of how to ask. Sometimes it seemed to him that girls spoke a different language, but he couldn't figure out when they'd learned it. He was pretty sure that they used to all speak the same language a year ago.

"We're talking about superstitions," said Leo. "Like how stepping where someone's grave is going to be makes them shudder involuntarily."

He always talked with big words, like a textbook. *Superstitions. Shudder. Involuntarily.* Some kids said it was because his mother was a part-time teacher over at the college, but Zach thought that was just how Leo was.

"Like stepping on a crack is supposed to break your mother's back?" Poppy asked. "I tried that when I was really little. I was so mad at Mom, but I don't even remember why now. Wait, no, I do remember! Nate pushed me in the backyard, and I whipped a branch at him. The branch got him good, right above the eye. He was bleeding like crazy, so even though he started it, I was the one who got in trouble. I stomped on cracks all up and down the block. And the next day, she slipped in the garden and sprained her ankle."

"No way," Leo said. Zach could see him mentally filing that away with all his other oddball stories.

Poppy laughed. "It's not like she actually broke her back. I mean, it was just a coincidence that she fell. But it scared me at the time. I thought I was some kind of powerful enchanter or something."

"And you avoided cracks for years after," Alice said. "Remember that? You would be crazy careful, always putting your feet sideways and going up on your tiptoes and stuff. You swerved around like a Roomba robot ballerina."

"Roombarina," Zach said automatically. For some reason, words were funnier smashed together.

"Roombarina," Alice echoed, spinning on one toe and then stumbling a little. "Exactly."

"That's a good portmanteau," said Leo. Zach nodded, the way he usually did when he had no idea what Leo was talking about.

They passed the old Episcopalian church with the big spire as they headed down Main Street. They walked past the barbershop, the pizza place where Zach had birthday parties when he was little, the bus station next to the post office, and the big old graveyard on the hill. Zach had followed this exact route many times, his fingers curled in his mother's when he was little and then gripping the handlebars of his bike when he was older, and now on foot to and from school. This was the town he'd grown up in, and even though it was small and a lot of the stores on Main Street were closed, even though windows were boarded up and rentals went unrented, Zach was used to the place.

He couldn't imagine living anywhere else, which was a real stumbling block in imagining running away.

"That stuff is real," Leo said. "For a while, my parents moved us around a lot, and there was this one apartment we lived in that was haunted. I swear—when

the ghost was in the room, the air would get really cold, even in the middle of summer. And there was one spot that was always ice-cold. You could put a space heater on top of it, and it wouldn't warm up. That's where somebody died. The landlady even said so."

"Did you ever actually see the ghost?" Alice asked.

Leo shook his head. "No, but sometimes he would move things. Like my mom's keys. Mom would yell for the ghost to give them back, and then, nine times out of ten, she'd find them right after. Mom says you have to know how to talk to ghosts or they'll walk all over you."

Poppy smiled like she did when she was anticipating

revealing something exciting—a twist to a story, a shocking turn, a villain's big move. Her cheeks were pink from the wind, and her eyes were bright. "Have you ever heard this one? When you drive past a cemetery, you have to hold your breath. If you don't, the spirits of the newly dead can get in your body through your mouth and then they can *possess* you."

Zach shivered, the hairs along his neck rising. Without meaning to, he imagined the taste of a ghost, like an acrid mouthful of smoke. He spat in the dirt, trying to untaste the idea.

"Ugh," Alice said into the silence that followed the end of Poppy's story. "You made me hold my breath! I was totally just trying not to inhale. Anyway, we already passed the graveyard—shouldn't you have told us the story before we passed it? Unless you wanted us to get possessed."

Zach thought again about the night before and the feeling of something right behind him, breathing on his neck, something that was about to reach out and grasp for him with its cold fingers. The story was like that, grabbing hold of him and promising that he'd think about it every time he was near a graveyard.

Poppy kept smiling. She made her eyes really wide and spoke in a flat, affectless tone. "Maybe I'm not Poppy anymore. Maybe I didn't know not to hold my breath and I learned the hard way. Maybe a spirit possessed me and now it's warning you, because it's too late. The spirits are already inside yooOOoooUUuu—"

"Come on, *stop*," Alice said, shoving Poppy's shoulder. They both began to laugh.

Leo laughed nervously along with them. "That's why it's a scary story. Because you can't do the one thing that would protect you—you'll never know if you held your breath long enough or let it out too soon. And you can't hold your breath forever."

"The smiling was creepy," said Zach. "Anyone tell you that you have a creepy smile, Poppy?"

She looked very pleased with herself.

They walked a few blocks more and then came to the place where Leo split off for home. He waved goodbye and headed off, cutting across a big lawn toward a trailer park.

Then it was just Alice and Poppy and Zach walking the few blocks to the development where their houses were clustered, all three nearly identical from the outside. His heart started to speed up again and his legs turned to lead because there was no way to avoid the conversation that was coming, even though he wanted to with all his might.

❧ CHAPTER FOUR ❧

THE AIR WAS COOL, THE TREES BRIGHT WITH YELLOW
and red leaves, and lawns thick with a wilted carpet
of brown. A gust of air shook the branches above
Zachary and blew his bangs over his eyes. He pushed
them back impatiently and looked up at the cloud-
less sky.

He thought of all of them—all his characters, stuck
in the duffel bag, rats chewing at the edges. He thought
of bugs crawling over them and trash dumped on top of
them. He thought of the folded-up Questions, still in
his backpack, and of how he'd said William's nightmare
was being buried alive.

"Hey," said Alice. "Do you guys want to meet up? I
have an idea for what might—"

"I can't," Zach said quickly. He'd planned out a whole speech the night before, lying on his back, staring up at the ceiling of his room, but he couldn't remember any of it now. He took a deep breath and blurted out the only thing he could think to say. "I don't want to play anymore."

Poppy frowned in confusion. "What are you talking about?"

For a moment, it seemed possible to take the words back, to tell Poppy and Alice what had really happened. He could explain what his dad had done and how angry he was and how he had no idea what to do now except be angry. He could tell them how he didn't want all the stories to remain unfinished. He could tell them how he felt like pieces of himself were gone, like part of him had been thrown out with his action figures.

"I've been really busy with school and basketball and everything," he said instead, his voice low. "I mean, you guys can keep playing or whatever."

"You mean ever? Like you don't want to play ever again?" When Poppy got upset, her neck would flush a blotchy red. He could see it coloring, as pink as her wind-whipped cheeks. She launched into a slightly desperate negotiation. "It's just that we're in the middle of something big. We came all the way through the

Gray Country and to the Blackest Sea. Couldn't we just finish this part?"

He'd been looking forward to crossing swords with the leader of the mermaids, who knew the way to an ancient underwater city full of secrets—including the secret to completing the Queen's quest and lifting her curse—plus there was the promise of fighting sharks. There were even hints that they might find a clue to William the Blade's parentage, plus the treasure of the Shark Prince—piles of gold and jewels so vast that Lady Jaye had been questing after it since she had first heard the story as an orphan beggar child. Remembering how awesome it was going to be made every new thought about playing hurt like the back of a shoe rubbing against a burst blister.

"We're too old anyway, don't you think?" he made himself say.

Alice looked stricken.

"That's stupid," Poppy said. "We weren't too old the day before yesterday."

"We were," Zach said.

"It's because of your friends on the team, isn't it?" Alice glanced over at Poppy, like maybe they'd had this conversation before. "You think they're going to find out and hassle you."

"I don't think anything." Zach sighed. "I just don't want to play anymore."

"You don't mean that," Poppy said.

He forced the words out. "I do."

"Maybe we could just take a break," Alice said slowly. "Do something else for a while."

"Sure," he said with a shrug.

"And then maybe if you change your mind . . ."

Zach thought about the time that Alice had first brought her Lady Jaye doll to a game—three months back. Before Lady Jaye, Alice's favorite character had been a Barbie named Aurora who had been raised by a herd of carnivorous horses. But one Monday morning, on the walk to school, Alice explained that she'd repainted an action figure from a thrift store over the weekend. She wanted to play somebody new.

Lady Jaye was different, all right. She was a thief who'd grown up on the streets of the biggest city in all their kingdoms, called Haven. And she didn't care about anything except for what she could steal and what fun she could have along the way.

Lady Jaye was crazy. She got a ride on William's ship because she wanted a ride to the Shark Prince's treasure, but every time he docked, Lady Jaye kept stealing from people, so they'd been banned from landing in at least five different places. William had to bail her out of situation after situation, until he finally got her to agree to stay aboard the *Neptune's Pearl*.

Except then she wound up doing things like climbing the mast with a blindfold on, just to show off. Alice's descriptions of Lady Jaye's antics had made Zach laugh so hard that his stomach hurt. His stomach hurt now, too, but for a different reason.

"I'm not going to change my mind," Zach said numbly.

"But it doesn't make any sense," Poppy said, not willing to let him off that easily. "You can't just stop. We're in the middle of a scene. What happens to everyone else? What happens to Lady Jaye? Even if she gets away from the mermaids, what then? What about the crew?"

William had promised Lady Jaye that he'd take her to the place marked on the map as the lair of the Shark Prince. He'd sworn it on his honor and on the *Neptune's Pearl*.

"Maybe one of your people can take over as captain." Zach hated the idea, but the *Neptune's Pearl* wasn't a particular toy that one of them owned. It was just a cutout piece of paper, and there was no reason for him to hang on to it.

"Maybe they'll make her walk the plank," said Poppy.

"I don't *care* what happens," Zach said, and all the simmering anger at his father, at this conversation, and at everything bled into his voice then, turning it cruel. "You figure it out. I don't care anymore."

"Okay," Alice said, holding up her hands like she was surrendering. "How about we walk over to the dirt mall? Or bike over. Whatever. See what's at the used bookstore and play the arcade games in the movie theater lobby. Like I said, a break."

Alice wasn't allowed there, so it was a generous offer.

"I don't really feel like it today," Zach said. "But thanks." They were almost to his street, almost home. He picked up his pace.

"Did you finish the Questions?" Poppy asked him.

He hitched his backpack higher on his shoulder and shook his head. The note was folded and tucked away in the front zippered pocket, scribbled on and illustrated, full of proof that he did care. He couldn't give it to her.

She held out her hand.

"I didn't answer them," he said. "What do you want?"

"Give me the paper back anyway. Maybe I'll make up my own answers."

He frowned. "I don't have them anymore. I lost them."

"You *lost* them?" Poppy yelled. He wondered if she was afraid of someone finding out what she'd asked. He would have been.

"They're probably just in your bag, right?" Alice said. "You could look."

"Sorry," Zach mumbled. "Like I said, I don't know where they are."

"What happened?" Poppy asked, grabbing his arm. "What's so different all of a sudden? Why are you so different?"

He turned to look at her. He had to get away before he said something that he couldn't take back. "I don't know. I don't want to play, that's all."

"Fine," Poppy said. "Just bring your people over one last time. One final time. So that they can say good-bye to our people."

"I can't," he said. "I just can't, Poppy."

"I just want to say good-bye." The hurt on Poppy's face was raw and so much like his own that it was hard to look at her. "They would want that. They'll miss Rose and Lady Jaye and Aeryn and Lysander, even if you don't."

"They're not real, you know." He knew he was being a jerk, but it felt good to lash out, even if was at the wrong person. "They're not real, and they can't want anything. Stop being such a loser. You can't play pretend forever."

Alice sucked in her breath. The red blotches on Poppy's neck had moved to her cheeks. She looked like she was about to cry or hit him; Zach wasn't sure which.

When she spoke, though, her voice was flat and grim. "The Queen—what if I take her out of the cabinet? I know where my mom keeps the key. I'll play her. She knows all the secrets, and she'll give you whatever you want. Everything. If you come tomorrow, you can have everything you want."

Zach hesitated. The Great Queen, who ruled over the Silver Hills, the Gray Country, the Land of the Witches, and the whole Blackest Sea. She would have information about William the Blade's father. With her blessing, all his crimes might be forgiven, his curse lifted, and William would be allowed to dock the *Neptune's Pearl* anywhere he wanted. It was a big thing for Poppy to promise—especially because her mother would be furious if Poppy actually took the doll out from the cabinet. The doll was very, very old, and—

according to Poppy's mother—worth a lot of money. She'd be worth a lot less if they touched her papery cotton dress or pawed at her brittle straw-gold curls. And if the Queen was free from her cage, then who knew what that meant for the world.

For a moment, he'd forgotten that there was no more game. It was an unpleasant shock to remember. No matter how tempting it was, Zach *couldn't* play. There was no William the Blade anymore.

"Sorry," he said, turning toward his house with a shrug.

Poppy made a strangled sound. Alice said something under her breath.

Zach bent his head, closed his eyes, and kept walking.

That night, at the kitchen table, Zach poked at his baked chicken. He wasn't hungry.

"Your mother pointed out to me that if I want you to start acting like a grown-up, I can't keep treating you like a kid," his father was saying, sounding overly sincere. "She's right. I shouldn't have tossed out your stuff, because it's my job to *guide* you toward the right choices, not make all those choices for you."

The tone in his father's voice made Zach think of

last year, when he'd gotten into a fight at school. His mother had made him sit in the principal's office until he was ready to tell Harry Parillo that he was sorry for punching him, even though Zach hadn't been sorry at all. Zach's father's apology sounded as forced as his had been.

"I know that it's hard to adjust to us being back together," Mom said. "But we're going to keep working on it. Zachary, do you have anything you want to say?"

"Nope," Zach said.

"That's okay," said his dad, getting up from the table and clapping Zach on the shoulder. "We understand each other, don't we?"

Awkward silence stretched between them.

Finally Zach nodded, because he did understand his father. He understood his wanting to make Mom happy. He understood not being sorry. It just didn't make Zach forgive him.

The next day, Zach went to practice and tried to blot out thoughts of Poppy and Alice and his father by playing ball so aggressively that he got lectured by his coach and benched for the rest of practice. He tried not to think about the story, which would go on without him, flowing around the empty spaces where his characters used to be until they were swallowed up and forgotten.

He thought again about running away, but the more time passed, the more he'd realized that he had nowhere to go.

Since his father was at the restaurant that night, his mother let him eat ravioli from a can on the couch in front of the television. They didn't talk much, although he caught her shooting him worried looks.

In the morning Zach asked her to drive him to school, and that afternoon he went home with Alex Rios. They played video games in Alex's finished basement on a bigger television than Zach had seen outside of a store.

The day after that, Alice walked up to Zach while he was shooting baskets at recess and pressed a note into his hand. A couple of the other guys yelled "Go ask Alice!" and "Somebody's got a girlfriend!" as she walked off, which made her hunch her shoulders like she was braced against a hard wind.

"Shut up," Zach said, shoving Peter Lewis, since he was standing closest.

"What?" Peter said. "I didn't say anything."

The note was folded up in a square this time, with his name carefully printed in blue ink. When he opened it, there were only three short sentences on the lined paper:

> Something happened with the Queen. Go to the hermit's place by the Silver Hills after school. It's <u>important</u>.

Important was underlined three times.

It's nothing, Zach told himself.

He thought of the Queen's fluttering lashes and the feeling of her closed eyes following him as he walked through the room.

The Queen wasn't real, though, so nothing important could have happened with her. This was just Poppy and Alice attempting to get him to show up so they could all have the same fight over again. They wanted him to play and he couldn't. There was nothing he could do except explain why it was over, and he couldn't bring himself to do that.

"What did the note say?" Alex asked. "She tell you that she wants your skinny body?"

Zach tore it in half and then in half again. "Nah. She just wants my math homework."

There was no practice after school that day, but he stayed late anyway, pretending there was. He managed to talk the coach into letting him shoot hoops in the gym, which he did methodically, alone, letting himself drown in the thump of the ball, the squeak of his sneakers, and the familiar smell of fresh floor wax and old sweat.

∽ CHAPTER FIVE ∾

ZACH WOKE IN THE DARKNESS OF HIS BEDROOM. HE wasn't sure why, but his heart raced, adrenaline pumping through his body, as though something had activated his body's fight-or-flight response. He blinked in the dark, letting his eyes adjust. The moon was high enough to give the room an eerie silvery glow. He could make out the familiar shapes of his furniture. His black cat was uncurling and stretching her long sleek body, claws digging into the coverlet. She padded up to him, her yellow eyes full of reflected light.

"What's up?" he whispered to The Party, reaching out to pet her soft triangular head and press his thumb against her ear, folding it down and rubbing it. She butted against him and started to purr.

Tap.

He jumped. The cat hissed, her white teeth flashing in the moonlight, and she jumped off the bed. Something small and hard had struck the window.

This was no echo of a dream, no made-up story. Something really had hit the glass, smacking against one of the panes he couldn't see, one of the lower ones, hidden behind blue half-curtains.

A sudden gust of wind made the branches outside shake and jitter. He couldn't help imagining the long, bony fingers of the trees scraping against the glass.

When he was a little kid, he'd had a firm belief in universally observed monster rules. He'd been sure, for example, that if he kept all parts of himself on the mattress and shrouded beneath blankets, if he kept his eyes closed, and if he pretended to be asleep, then he'd be safe. He didn't know where he'd gotten the idea from. He *did* remember his mother saying he'd smother himself if he kept sleeping with his head under the comforter. Then one night—quite randomly—he fell asleep with his head above the covers like a normal person, and no monster got him. Over time he got spottier about observing his safety precautions, until he routinely slept with an arm dangling off the side of his bed and his feet kicked free of the sheets.

But right then, at the sound of the wind, for one panicky moment, all he wanted was to burrow under the blankets and never come out.

Tap. Tap.

The thing hitting the window was just a branch, he told himself.

Or an insomniac squirrel rattling around in the gutters.

Or a neighbor cat trying to pick a fight with The Party.

Tap.

He was never going to be able to go back to sleep if he didn't look. Zach slid out of bed, his bare feet padding over the carpet. Steeling himself and taking a deep breath, he pushed aside the curtain.

There were a few scattered pebbles on the roof tiles in front of his window. That was the first thing he noticed. The second was that when he looked past the roof, he saw two dark figures looking up at him from the moonlit lawn. He was too surprised to shout. They had windblown hair and upturned faces and, for a moment, he didn't know them. But then he realized it was only Poppy and Alice, not zombie girls or witches or ghosts. Alice lifted her hand in a shy wave. Poppy had another handful of pebbles and looked ready to throw them at him.

He let out his breath and waved back a little unsteadily. His hammering heart started to slow.

Poppy beckoned to him. *Come down,* she was signaling.

He thought of the note that Alice had passed him and the way she'd underlined *important,* but he couldn't think of anything so important that it would lead them to sneak out of their houses on a Friday night. Alice's grandmother would ground her for the rest of forever if she found out.

Zach backed away from the window. Quietly he went to the closet and pushed his feet into a pair of sneakers. He pulled a sweater over his T-shirt and crept downstairs in his alligator pajama bottoms.

The Party followed, mewling plaintively, probably hoping to be fed.

The under-cabinet lights in the kitchen were bright enough to stumble through by, and he managed to find his coat on a hook in the entranceway. The microwave showed the time in blinking green numbers: three minutes past midnight. Zach shouldered his coat on and went outside, closing the door before the cat could slip through.

Poppy and Alice were waiting for him.

"Hey," he whispered into the dark. "What's going on? What happened?"

"Shhhhh," Poppy said. "You'll wake up everyone. Come on."

"Where to?" he asked, looking back at his house. There was a light on in his parents' bedroom upstairs. Sometimes his mother stayed up late to read; sometimes she fell asleep with the light on. If she was still awake, the sound of them talking might carry up to her, but he wanted to know *something* before he just followed Alice and Poppy into the night.

"The Silver Hills," Alice said.

That was a junkyard that specialized in metal about half a mile from their houses. The owner bought everything from car parts to tin cans and, although no one was sure what he did with them other than let them rust in huge mounds on his property, they were a pretty impressive sight. The stripped rods, machine parts, and batteries gleamed like mountains of silver, so that's why they'd started calling it the Silver Hills. They'd come up with a whole story line, including dwarves and trolls and a princess doll that Poppy had painted silver.

Zach jogged behind Poppy and Alice, the wind cutting through his thin pajamas, making him feel both cold and sort of ridiculous. After a few minutes Poppy pulled a flashlight out of her jacket and clicked it on. It illuminated only a narrow patch of grass and dirt, so she had to swing it back and forth to see much.

There was the same old high chain-link fence around the property that Zach remembered. And there was the same old abandoned shed that they'd found a few summers ago and used as a clubhouse until Alice's grandmother had found out about it and given them a speech about tetanus and how it led to something she called lockjaw. Zach wasn't sure lockjaw was a real thing, but he thought about it every time his neck felt stiff.

They hadn't been there since—or at least, *he* hadn't. He wondered if Poppy and Alice snuck out to the shed without him. They seemed full of secrets tonight. The only secret he had was one he wished he didn't.

Alice opened the creaky old door and went inside. He followed nervously.

Poppy sat down on the splintery floor, cross-legged, setting the flashlight against her sneakers, so it lit her face. Then she unhooked her backpack from one shoulder, pulling it around onto her lap.

"So are you going to tell me what's going on?" Zach asked, sitting down across from Poppy. The wood planks were cold under his pajama pants, and he shifted, trying to get comfortable.

Doll Bones

She unzipped her bag. "You're going to laugh," she said. "But you shouldn't."

He glanced over at Alice. She was leaning against one wall of the shed. "Poppy saw a ghost," she said.

He tried to suppress a shudder. Ghosts weren't something you talked about in an abandoned shed at night. "You're just trying to freak me out. This is some kind of stupid—"

Poppy carefully took the bone china doll from her backpack. Zach drew in his breath and went silent. The Queen's dull black eyes were open, her gaze boring into his own. He'd always thought she was creepy-looking, but in the reflected beam of the flashlight, she seemed demonic.

Poppy touched the doll's face. It was pure white, like a dinner plate. Hair, dry as brush bristles, was threaded into her scalp, and her cheeks and lips were rouged a faint pink. When she was tilted onto her back, her eyes stayed open instead of closing the way they should have, as though she was still watching Zach. There was a tear at the shoulder of her thin, brittle gown and tiny pinholes through the discolored fabric. It hadn't aged as well as the rest of the doll— and the ride in Poppy's backpack probably hadn't helped.

"The Queen," Zach said unsteadily, forcing a sneer into his voice to cover his rising fear. "So what? You brought me all the way out here to see a *doll*?"

"Just listen," Alice said. "Try not to be the huge jerk you've turned into."

Alice never said stuff like that, especially not to him. It stung.

"I know you told us you weren't going to come over the other day, but I thought you might anyway," Poppy said, talking fast. "And I couldn't just go in the cabinet and get the Queen if Mom was there. So I took the doll out of the case that night when we had the argument and moved around some of Mom's other stuff to hide what I'd done. But that night—well, I saw the dead girl."

"You mean you had a *nightmare*," Zach said.

"Just shut up a minute," said Alice.

"It wasn't like a regular dream," Poppy said, her fingers smoothing back the Queen's curls and her voice changing, going soft and chill as the night air. It reminded Zach of the way Poppy talked when she played villains or even the Queen herself. "It wasn't like dreaming at all. She was sitting on the end of my bed. Her hair was blond, like the doll's, but it was tangled and dirty. She was wearing a nightdress smeared with mud. She told me I had to bury her. She said she couldn't rest until her bones were in her own grave, and if I didn't help her, she would make me sorry."

Poppy paused, as though she was expecting him to say something sarcastic. Alice shifted uncomfortably. Zach was silent for a long moment, arrested by the images Poppy had conjured. He could almost see the girl in her stained nightgown.

"Her *bones*?" he finally echoed.

"Did you know that bone china has real bones in it?" Poppy said, tapping a porcelain cheek. "Her clay was made from human bones. Little-girl bones. That hair threaded through the scalp is the little girl's hair. And the body of the doll is filled with her leftover ashes."

A shiver ran up his spine. He closed his eyes to keep from looking at the doll in Poppy's lap. "Okay, this is your idea of a funny prank. I get it. You're mad at me for not playing the game anymore, so you made up this story to scare me. What's the punch line? Did one of you rig a sheet outside to flutter from a tree or something?"

"I told you," Alice said to Poppy, under her breath.

"You really *did* rig a sheet?" Zach frowned, looking out at the trees and the mounds of cans and metal.

"No, idiot," said Alice. "I told her that you wouldn't believe us and that you wouldn't want to help."

He threw up his hands in confusion. "Help with

what? Help you *bury* a *doll*? Why would you need to wake me up in the middle of the night to help you do that?"

Poppy pulled the doll to her chest, and one of the eyes closed and opened, as though it was winking at him. "Eleanor Kerchner is real. That's the doll-girl's name. She told me about herself. Her father was some kind of worker for a china manufacturer, designing and decorating pottery, and when Eleanor died, her dad went totally crazy. He couldn't bear to put her in the ground, so he took her body back to the kilns at his job, chopped her up, and cremated her. He ground up her burnt bones and used them to make a batch of bone china, then poured it into a mold cast from one of Eleanor's favorite dolls. So her grave stayed empty."

Zach tried to swallow, although his throat suddenly felt very dry. It was too easy to imagine the doll moving on her own, fluttering her painted eyelids and turning toward him. Maybe opening her tiny rosebud of a mouth to scream. "She told you that?"

"Each night she told me a little bit more of her story." Illuminated by the flashlight, Poppy's face had become strange. "She's not going to rest until we bury her. And she's not going to let us rest either. She promised to make us miserable unless we help her."

He looked at Alice. "And you believe it? You believe all of this?"

"I never believed in ghosts, so not at first," Alice said. "No offense, Poppy, but it's a crazy story. And I'm still not totally sure, but show him the *thing*. It's pretty convincing."

"Show me what?"

Poppy pulled the doll's head sharply up from the body. Zach gasped at the sudden violence of it, but all that it revealed was a string-and-rusty-metal-hook apparatus. With a twist, the Queen's head came entirely off, leaving the hook still attached to the neck, hanging from the cord. Poppy slid her fingers into the body of the doll, feeling around like she was trying to reach something.

"What are you doing?" He stared at the disembodied head resting on Poppy's knee. The eyes were closed now.

Poppy drew out an old burlap bag from the neck cavity. "Here, take this and look inside."

He took the rough cloth as she turned the beam of the flashlight on it, revealing letters and a date in blocky print. The bag was full, but Zach couldn't tell what it was full with.

"Liverpool?" he read out loud. He had a vague memory of the place from some late-night British rock documentary his mom had been watching. "That's where the Beatles are from—in England. There's no way we can go there. I guess we're going to have to find out if ghost girls really can curse people, because—"

"That's what I thought at first," Alice said, and pointed to the markings. "But look again. It says *East* Liverpool. In *Ohio*. So we could get on a bus and be there by morning." She paused. "And we are. We're going. Tonight. Well, technically, it's morning, so we're going in the morning."

He looked from the doll to Alice and then to Poppy. "This is why you brought me out here?"

"We tried to explain yesterday," Alice said. "I told you it was important."

Poppy reached down and turned the flashlight beam on her watch, then shone it at him. "There's a bus stopping in town at two fifteen in the morning. It's coming from Philadelphia and going to Youngstown. One of the stops is East Liverpool. Alice said she'd come if you would too."

Zach thought about the ghost story that Poppy had told on their last walk home, the one about holding your breath when you passed a cemetery. Was she trying to play a different kind of game? A game that she was making out of their real lives? But Poppy didn't look gleeful, the way she did when she had a thrilling idea. She looked pale and nervous, like she hadn't been sleeping well.

"You'll really go?" he asked finally, looking at Alice. Her grandmother wouldn't like a single thing about this: not the ghost, not the bus, definitely not Alice being out at two in the morning with a boy—even if the boy was just him.

Alice shrugged.

Zach's parents wouldn't like him going either, but that was a point in favor of the plan, as far as he was concerned. And if he decided that he never wanted to come back, well, at least he'd have some company while he figured out where he was going. In stories, orphan boys became assistant pig keepers and magician's apprentices. In real life, he wasn't sure there were any equivalent jobs.

"You still haven't looked in the bag," Alice said, pointing to the burlap sack he was holding. "It's pretty weird."

With trepidation, he pulled the drawstrings so that he could peer inside. Poppy handed Alice the flashlight. She held it up high, pointing it down at him.

For a moment, Zach didn't know what he was seeing. The bag seemed to be full of something that looked a little bit like dark sand with chunks of shells in it. Then he realized that the bag was full of gray ash, and what he'd thought were shells were actually sharp, pale pieces of bone.

Of course. The leftover ashes. The remains of a ghost. Of a girl. Of the Queen.

A nameless primal terror washed over him. He wanted to drop the bag, wanted to race out of the shed and go back to bed where he could shiver under his own covers. But he didn't move. His hands started to shake, and he drew the strings tight so he didn't have to look anymore.

"Poppy thinks we can catch a bus back in the afternoon and be home by dinnertime. It's only a three-hour ride, but there aren't a lot of buses from here to there—just this one early in the morning, and another in the afternoon that gets in too late for us to ride back in time. We left a note for her parents." Despite her words, Alice's voice grew a little uncertain. Zach wondered if she'd balked at first, before she'd apparently promised Poppy that if he went, she would go too.

"If these bones are *real*," he began, "shouldn't we tell someone? A girl died. Maybe Eleanor's father murdered her. Maybe it's some kind of cold-case file."

"No one's going to care about some old story,"

Poppy said. "And even if they did, they'd just take the doll away from us—put her in a museum or display her somewhere—and then her spirit would be angry."

He paused, considering everything she'd said and also what she hadn't said. "Did you find the ashes before or after you dreamed about Eleanor Kerchner?"

"I'm going whether you both come or not," Poppy said, snatching the burlap bag out of his hand. He guessed that meant she'd found the ashes first. "Whether you believe me or not, I'm going to bury her like she wants."

Getting on a bus in the middle of the night to a place they'd never been was daunting. It also seemed a little bit like an adventure.

"Okay," he said. "Fine. I'll come."

Alice looked at him in wide-eyed surprise. He wondered for the first time if she'd been planning on him saying no and hadn't considered the possibility that he'd say yes. If so, she probably should have told him.

"I'll come," he continued, "so long as you both promise not to ask me about the game or why I don't want to play. Okay? No more hassling me about it."

"Okay," said Poppy.

"Okay," said Alice.

"*Okay,*" said Zach.

"You need to get ready fast," Poppy said. "And

leave a note so your parents don't freak out. Just tell them you got up early and that you'll be back tonight."

"And you're sure the bus will get us back in time?" Alice asked. "You're positive?"

"Yes," Poppy said. "I planned it all out. Just bring food and supplies, okay, Zach? We'll meet at the mailbox in twenty minutes."

She switched off the flashlight and, for a moment, the shed was plunged into darkness.

Zach blinked, willing his eyes to adjust. By the time they did, Poppy had put away the Queen, so at least her terrible head with its winking eye was hidden.

Zach walked home through the hushed streets, his sneakers wet with dew from the frosted grass. There was a kind of quiet that hung over the world in the middle of the night, as though there was no one else awake anywhere. It felt ripe with magic and endless possibility.

He snuck back into his house and stood for a long moment in the dark kitchen, a feeling of great daring swelling his heart. When he finally went to the cabinets, he felt as though he was provisioning himself for one of those epic fantasy quests—the kind that required a lot of jerky or something called hardtack that he'd read about soldiers eating during the Civil War and which he thought might be a kind of bread. His mother didn't have either of those things, nor did she have elven lembas, which had kept Frodo and Sam from starving on the way to Mount Doom and always made him think of matzoh (which his mom also didn't have). He did find a can of orange soda, a package of saltine crackers, three oranges, red Twizzlers, and a jar of peanut butter, all of which he stuffed into his backpack.

In his room, Zach changed into jeans, switched out his sweater for a zip-up sweatshirt, and packed a few other random things he thought he might need: twenty-three dollars (twenty of which had come from his aunt in a card for his birthday), a book identifying poisonous plants (in case they needed to live in the wild and eat berries, which admittedly seemed like a remote possibility), and a sleeping bag that was a little too small for him but worked okay as a blanket when completely unzipped. In the hall closet, he found a flashlight, and he picked up a garden spade from beside the back door.

Before he left, he wrote out the note and propped it up on his bed. It read:

Got up early. Gone to play basketball. Might not be back for dinner.

Might not be back forever, he thought, but didn't write.

As he left the house, closing the door quietly behind him, he wondered, for a moment, again, if this was a trick. A lie. Poppy's attempt at one last game.

But the ashes had seemed real, he reminded himself.

In the end, he wasn't sure if he went because he half believed in the ghost already or because he was used to following Poppy's lead in a story or simply because leaving allowed him to run away and still believe he could come back.

If he wanted.

❧ CHAPTER SIX ❧

ZACHARY WAS USED TO STORIES WITHOUT HAPPY END-
ings. His dad called where they lived West of Nowhere,
Pennsylvania, claiming it bordered Better off Forgotten,
West Virginia, and Already Forgotten, Ohio. When
Zach was little, those had seemed like magical place
names, before he realized they were just sarcasm. Zach's
mother had gone to school to be an art therapist, but the
only place she could get work was in a juvenile detention
center. If she wanted the kids there to do art, she had
to bring the supplies and collect them after each session
because her supervisor was afraid of the kids jabbing each
other's eyes out with markers.

Zach's mother's parents, now living permanently in
Florida, would tell stories about how things used to be.

About how the big Victorian houses—the ones built by some famous architect, the ones that were in the center of town—used to be owned by single families and not divided into run-down apartments. His grandmother told stories about the people she'd known when she was a little girl, people who got out of town and made it elsewhere. The happiest the stories got were when his parents talked about how things were going to get better, although neither one of them really seemed to believe it, and Zach didn't believe it anymore either.

When Zach's dad left three years ago, he said he was going to run his own restaurant in Philadelphia and he was going to Italy to study how pasta was really made and he was getting a late-night spot on a local cable channel and would parlay that into a fortune. But two months later, he moved back and into one of the crappy apartments in the biggest and worst-kept Victorian and drifted in and out of Zach's life, until he finally drifted back to their house. It was as if the town had some kind of gravitational influence on the people who lived there. But even as Zach thought that, he knew it was just another story. Dad was back because he hadn't been able to hack it in the city. That was all.

He wondered whether growing up was learning that most stories turned out to be lies.

The bus stop was cold enough that Zach's breath clouded in the air. The wind had picked up. It washed over them as they huddled together against the brick exterior of the post office. In the flickering streetlight, Zach could see the girls better. Poppy had pulled back her coppery hair into a ponytail and was wearing a dark-green sweater with jeans and tall brown boots. Alice was in a big shapeless red coat. Both of them had backpacks slung over their shoulders.

He felt his gaze going to Poppy's backpack, knowing the Queen was inside and knowing, without knowing how he knew, that her eyes were open. He felt the weight of her stare on his back when he turned away. The hairs on the back of his neck stuck up, tickling his skin and making him shiver.

The bus was already fifteen minutes late, and there was no sign of it—or any other vehicle—on the road. A while back they'd seen a police car from a way off and had pressed themselves against the wall of the building. As they hid, Poppy muttered the whole time about the vividness of Alice's coat giving them away and Alice muttered back about how she'd just packed for a sleepover because she hadn't thought they were taking off somewhere harebrained *that very night*. But the police car had turned onto Main Street and away from them. And the next car that passed was a truck. It didn't even slow.

Alice yawned. "Maybe we should go back. It doesn't look like the bus is coming."

Zach, impelled by the impulse that makes yawns catch, yawned too.

"*Stop,*" Poppy said. "We just have to wait a little longer."

"You can't be mad at us for being tired," Zach said.

Poppy was clearly still upset, but she didn't argue with him. "We'll sleep on the bus."

Alice bit her lip and looked hopefully at the stretch of empty road. She looked happier the longer they waited. Zach was pretty sure she was betting on the bus not coming and the three of them going back to their beds, having had a nice little middle-of-the-night adventure. He could tell Alice didn't want to be the one who chickened out, but she obviously also didn't want to go. If Alice's grandmother found out about any of this, there would be no more play practice, no more sleepovers, no more chance of hanging out with Zach or Poppy. Ever.

Zach understood all that and he felt bad for her, but not bad enough to say anything. Selfishly, he wanted her along.

"Two more minutes," said Alice, "and then we go back. I'm freezing."

Poppy didn't reply.

"One minute, fifty-nine seconds," Alice said. "One minute, fifty-eight seconds."

Looking at the bus stop sign, Zach thought about what it would be like to get off at a place like this in a different town, one he had no idea how to navigate. "When we get to East Liverpool, you know where we're supposed to go, right? What cemetery Eleanor is supposed to be buried in and how to find the grave. You know all that, right?"

Poppy opened her mouth and hesitated over the answer. Just then a bus turned the corner three blocks away, washing them with its headlights. He didn't realize how worried Poppy had been that it wasn't coming until he saw how relieved she looked as the bus drew closer. Alice's face froze in an expression of dread.

"You don't have to go," he whispered to her, deciding he could be only so much of a jerk.

"No," she said, looking back down the street, away from the bus, and sighing. "It's not that. I'm just tired. Anyway, if I snuck back into my house when I'm supposed to be sleeping at Poppy's, Grandma would have a lot of questions."

The last time Alice had gotten busted for staying out after curfew, she'd gotten grounded for a solid month. She'd been to the movie version of one of her favorite musicals, along with some of her theater friends and Poppy. Somehow the parent who was giving them a ride didn't come on time, or maybe it took too long to drop everybody off, but Alice wound up home a half hour late. That was all it took. Boom. She was in mega-trouble. No phone calls. No Internet. No nothing.

So even though he knew that she wasn't telling the whole truth about wanting to go, given that she was likely to get in trouble either way, he figured she might as well have an adventure and hope for the best.

The door opened with a creak of gears. An old man with a short white beard looked down at them. A small gold hoop hung from one of his ears, and he had a face that reminded Zach of a gruff and unfriendly wizard. "Well, get on if you're getting on."

Poppy, Zach, and Alice climbed the steps, each feeding cash into a machine beside the driver. It printed three tickets and dispensed change into a bowl with a clatter. Zach shuffled down the aisle, past a knitting woman and three college-age guys asleep in their seats, past a guy muttering to himself and looking out the window.

Zach went all the way to the back of the bus, following Poppy. They sat in the long last seat. A moment later Alice joined them, squeezing in next to the window.

"See," Poppy said, pulling her legs up, so that she was sitting on her feet in a weird yoga pose. "Everything's going according to plan."

"I can't believe the bus actually came," Alice said faintly.

Zach looked at Poppy's backpack resting on the floor and wondered whether Poppy had reattached the Queen's head or whether it would roll around in the bottom of her bag when the bus turned corners. He thought he could see a few threads of her blond hair peeking out from where the zipper wasn't fully closed.

The bus lurched forward, pulling away from the bus stop, and despite everything, Zach started to grin. They were leaving home by themselves—going on a real adventure, the kind that changed you. He felt a thrill run through him.

"You never really answered me before," Zach said. "Do you know where the cemetery is? Do you know where we're going, Poppy?"

"The grave is under a willow tree. Eleanor will tell us the rest."

"Eleanor will tell us?" he asked in a quiet, urgent voice.

"She told me this much, didn't she?" Poppy answered, and then in that way she had, where Zach was sure she wasn't right yet somehow she seemed right, she added neatly and unanswerably, "If you didn't believe me, why did you come?"

Exasperated, he mimed banging his head against the back of the seat. Poppy ignored him.

Alice leaned against the window and pulled her legs up onto the seat, resting one shoe against Zach's leg. She looked exhausted, but no longer unhappy. "I'm going to try to sleep."

He rested a hand on her ankle so it wouldn't slip.

"We should take shifts," Poppy said. "Keep watch. Like you're supposed to on a quest. So we don't miss our stop."

"Okay," Zach said, sticking out a fisted hand. "Rock, paper, scissors."

Alice held out her hand and blinked muzzily, like she was trying to stay awake. She still beat him, throwing rock to his scissors. He stuck with scissors and tricked Poppy, who threw paper, expecting him to change moves. And then Alice beat Poppy, sticking Poppy with first watch, Zach with second, and Alice, third. Zach rested his head against his own backpack and closed his eyes.

He didn't think he'd be able to go to sleep, but he must have dozed off, because it seemed like moments later he awoke to Poppy's sharp yelp.

He sat up. The old guy who'd been talking to himself had moved to the seat in front of them. He was leaning close to Poppy and just letting go of a strand of her hair.

"I was just kidding you. Come on, you're a cute little thing. Ain't you used to being teased?" His bad breath washed over Zach, bringing with it a moldering smell, like wet clothes left in the washing machine overnight and sneakers after a long game. His hair was wild tangled curls, shot through with gray, and he had a scraggly beard hiding half of his windblown face. Nicotine stains darkened the ends of his pale fingers. "That your brother? Don't he tease you?"

"Yes, he's my brother," Poppy lied quickly. "And he doesn't like it if I talk to strangers."

He cackled, revealing a black gap where a few bottom teeth should have been. He turned his attention to Zach. "I was just telling your smart-mouth little sister here that you can't be sure this bus is going to take you where you want to go." He sounded teasing all right, but in a bad way. A scary way. "That bus driver—you can't trust him. He's senile as a moose. And sometimes he gets aliens in him."

Alice shifted and opened her eyes, blinking away dreams. When she saw the old guy, her eyes went wide and she grabbed for her bag. "What's going on?"

"Okay," Zach told the man, leaning forward, trying to get between him and Poppy. His father would say that as the boy, it was his responsibility to protect the girls. That made him even more scared, because he was afraid he'd let them down. "Thanks for the advice."

The old guy's grin widened. "Oh, the little man is going to give Tinshoe Jones the brush-off. You want to fight? You want to show off for them girls? And who is that one over there? She's no sister of yours. Just what is it that you three are doing, anyway? Running off from home?"

Alice leaned forward. "We're not doing anything."

"Look, we appreciate you coming over and talking with us," Poppy said placatingly. "But if that's all—"

"Senile as all get out." Tinshoe tapped his head and made a swirly motion with his finger, returning to what seemed to be his favorite subject—the bus driver. "Crazy as anything. Sometimes he gets a little lost. Sometimes he just parks and gets out of the bus, wanders around for a while. And sometimes he has meetings with them— them *things*. In their shiny spaceship. You can see the lights. Just leaves us out here for as long as it takes him to communicate."

Alice elbowed Zach and raised her eyebrows, eyes wide.

"Okay," Poppy said. "We'll watch out for that."

"You've got real pretty hair too," Tinshoe Jones said, turning to Alice with a sly grin. His fingers darted out to tug at one of her braids. "Like little ropes."

Alice jerked back.

"Don't touch her," Zach said.

"Oh, possessive, huh? Well then, what if I talk with your sister and leave the two of you alone?" Tinshoe grabbed for Poppy's arm. She pushed herself back against the cushion and out of the range of his hand before he could touch her.

"Hey!" Zach said.

The man laughed. "You all are real jumpy, you know that? Real paranoid. Well, I'm not gonna talk to the blonde, so you better forget that idea. I don't like the way she's looking at me. She's going to tell you that she'd never hurt anybody, but don't you listen. She'd hurt you, all right. She'd hurt you and she'd like it."

None of them were blond. In fact, as far as Zach could tell, no one on the bus was blond. He wondered what it was like to be so crazy that you actually saw things that weren't there. He wondered if when you hallucinated, the stuff you were imagining was just as clear as regular stuff, or if it was hazy at the edges, so that if you really concentrated, you could tell.

"It's time for you to sit somewhere else," Alice told him, drawing herself up impressively, like she did onstage at the school play. "I might not look like it, but I am their sister. I'm adopted. And I don't want you to talk to my brother like that anymore."

"Aw, c'mon," he said, reaching into his front breast pocket and coming out with a small paper-bag-wrapped bottle. "I have a black belt. You'll need me when the aliens come."

The bus turned a corner and started to slow. There was a brightly lit bus station up the road. Zach let out a sigh of relief.

"You wait and see. That driver's gonna roll on out of this bus and leave all of us alone, and when he comes back, he's going to have a new face. The aliens ride around in his skin. So when he does that, who are you going to tell?"

The rest of the bus was quiet and dark, the only

lights in two strips down the center aisle and near the front, where the knitting lady sat. It seemed like a vast distance. There was only the click of her needles and the sound of the man's voice.

In just a couple of minutes, they would be able to get off the bus, but what then? It was too soon for this to be East Liverpool. This was just a random stop in a random town they didn't know.

"You be careful," Tinshoe Jones said, looking right at Zach. "You better not let them get taken. That's your job as the brother. You the man in the family, and you got to fight to make sure the aliens don't steal their faces. Aliens like red hair. They take you down in them diamond ghost caves and you never come out again."

"But aliens don't live underground," Alice said, completely incapable of not pointing out when something didn't make sense. "They live in the sky. In spaceships."

Zach widened his eyes, trying to signal her not to say anything that would agitate Tinshoe Jones.

The bus stopped, its engine grinding. The door opened and the overhead lights came on, making Tinshoe's skin look sallow. He took a swig from the paper-bag-covered bottle. Then he stood up.

"Shows what you know. No, the safest thing is for you all to stay right here on the bus."

They looked at one another.

"I've got to use the bathroom," Zach said.

"Then you go," Tinshoe Jones said. "I'll protect these ladies and make sure you got the same face you left with."

"What if *we* need to protect *him*?" Alice asked, standing up.

Tinshoe Jones shook his head. "You can't go where he's going."

For a horrible moment Zach worried that Tinshoe Jones was going to block the aisle and make it impossible for them to exit. But then the bus driver stood up and turned his head toward them. Zach let out a sigh of relief.

If Tinshoe Jones knew the driver well enough to complain about him constantly stopping for aliens, he must take this route a lot. And if he took this route, he must have harassed passengers before. The bus driver would come back, say a few things, and Tinshoe Jones would go back to his seat. Everything would work out.

But the driver just took a long look at Zach, Poppy, and Alice and got off the bus. He didn't say or do a single thing to help them.

Tinshoe Jones wore a smirk on his face like he'd known all along he wasn't going to get in trouble.

Poppy shoved past him with a suddenness that got her through before he could react. While Tinshoe Jones gaped at her, Zach charged down the aisle, catching Alice's hand and pulling her with him. Tinshoe Jones grabbed for Alice, and she gave a single, blood-curdling shriek, loud enough for the frat boys to wake up and the knitting lady to turn around in her seat. Loud enough for Tinshoe to let Alice go in surprise.

"Don't come crying to me when the aliens take your faces!" he yelled after them.

The bus driver was smoking a cigarette, talking to two station employees, when they charged past him and into the building. There were benches and vending machines and bright fluorescent lights. Alice collapsed onto a bench, her eyes a little wet. She looked as freaked out as Zach felt.

"What are we going to do?" Poppy asked, pacing back and forth, backpack over one shoulder.

"This was your plan," Zach said, and then regretted it. He knew he wasn't being fair, but he was tired and upset and had no idea what to do himself. He felt useless.

"We can't get back on that bus," said Alice.

"Maybe we could tell someone—like a cop. There has to be a cop around a late-night bus station, right?"

"Yeah, and they'll ask us how old we are." Alice shook her head. "And call our families. No."

Zach looked over at the bus driver. One station employee was speaking into a walkie-talkie. The other was watching the three of them.

"I think we have to get out of here," Zach said.

"Why?" asked Alice. Then she noticed the three men standing together and got up quickly, swinging her bag onto her shoulder.

Zach took Poppy's arm. "Right now. C'mon. Go."

"But we didn't do anything," Poppy said, walking along with him. "Why would they be after us? Why not do something about that guy? He's the one—"

"Because we're kids," Zach whispered, cutting her off.

"We're being too obvious," Alice said under her breath. "Poppy, we should go into the girls' room and sneak out from there. Zach, meet us outside. Get something from the vending machine. Everyone, go slow."

Zach took a deep breath and then spoke loudly and as casually as he could, "I'll meet you guys back on the bus."

Alice smiled and nodded exaggeratedly, playing casual too now. Poppy tried to follow her lead.

One of the bus station employees had peeled away from the others and was heading in Zach's direction,

his shoe falls echoing in the mostly empty space. He wasn't rushing, but he had too much purpose in the way he moved to be just strolling. Zach started toward the door, deliberately not running despite wanting to. He paused a minute to look at the vending machine. In its reflection, he saw the station guy drawing closer, his blue uniform making him seem ominously authoritative.

Zach moved toward the door.

"Hey you, there," the station guy called to him.

But Zach was out through the doors and turning a

corner of the building and seeing Alice lowering herself from the girls' bathroom window. Poppy jumped out after her and they were off and running into the darkness of an unknown town.

☙ CHAPTER SEVEN ☙

THEY HUDDLED IN THE DARK BEHIND A TATTOO PARLOR and watched as the bus pulled out of the station in a cloud of exhaust, taking with it both the crazy guy and their chances of getting to East Liverpool by morning. All the adrenaline Zach had felt back in the station burned off of him, and he felt tired down to the marrow of his bones. Eye-droopingly exhausted. He leaned against the brick wall and wondered if it was possible to fall asleep standing up.

"Where are we?" Alice asked finally, her breath clouding in the air.

"And how are going to get out of here?" asked Zach, pushing off from the wall. "We don't even know what town we're in."

Poppy followed. "There's only two buses to East Liverpool that take this route, and if we wait to take the next one—in the afternoon—then we won't have enough time to take the bus back by tonight."

"Forget East Liverpool. We've got to get home," Alice said, digging out the cell phone that she was only allowed to use for emergencies.

"Sure," Zach said. "But we can't do that, either, can we?"

Poppy pulled the bus schedule from one of her pockets, along with a raggedy map. "You can look at this stuff if you want, but it's not going to tell you anything I haven't already told you."

Alice took the bus schedule and opened it, studying the names of stations as though she were going to be able to figure out where they were just by finding a name that struck her as feeling like the right one.

"Hold on," Zach said, walking the other way down the alley, so that he could see the front of the bus station. He walked back again. "East Rochester. There's a sign that says so—but where *is* that?"

Poppy crowded next to Alice, so they were squinting together at the schedule in the dim moonlight. "There were only two more stops before East Liverpool," Poppy said finally. "We almost made it."

"We're not even out of Pennsylvania yet," said Alice. "We didn't almost make anything."

Poppy unfolded the map and tapped it grandly. "Look, *that* says Ohio." Then she shook her head. "Oh, it says Ohio *River*."

Alice pulled her coat more tightly around her, sitting down on the back steps of a building. Dumpsters loomed to one side of her. "Can you call Tom and see if he'll pick us up?" Her voice sounded on the verge of panic. Calm, but not likely to stay that way.

Poppy just looked at her. "My brother will never come all the way here. Not in that junker car of his."

"Your sister, then?" Alice asked, chewing on the end of one of her braids.

Poppy shook her head. "She broke her phone and hasn't gotten a new one yet. I couldn't get ahold of her if I wanted to."

Alice looked at the face of her phone, frowning. "I guess I could call my aunt Linda. She'd be mad, but she'd come."

"Would she tell your grandmother?" Zach asked.

Alice sighed heavily, a little shudder going across her shoulders. "Probably. And then I'll get grounded forever and have to quit the play and be totally miserable. But what else are we going to do?"

Zach tried to imagine a single thing they could tell Alice's grandmother to try and make sense of what they'd done. She wouldn't want to hear about a creepy, possibly-still-headless doll, a ghost, and a curse that, more likely than not, didn't even exist.

"I won't go back," Poppy said, sitting on the steps next to Alice. "I'm going to wait for the next bus and keep going."

"But you said that the next bus wasn't coming until the afternoon, so you won't make it home before Sunday," Alice said. "Where would you sleep?"

Poppy took a deep but unsteady breath. Zach could see that the idea of Alice leaving her made Poppy feel a lot less daring. He didn't want Alice to go either; she was good at making crazy ideas actually work. If Poppy came up with the idea that they needed an ancient temple under the waves, Alice was the one who would actually find the discarded chunks of concrete to build it. Her going home would pretty much signal that they were doing something dumb.

"Alice is right. We can bury the Queen next weekend or the weekend after that," Zach said. "What's the difference?"

Poppy's shoulders hunched forward as she got more tense. "If we don't keep going now, we'll never do it. We just won't. You guys will make excuses and I'll chicken out and Eleanor will find someone else to haunt, because I won't be interesting enough to have a ghost talk to me. I won't deserve to be the hero of a story, and I won't be one."

"Everyone has a story," Alice murmured. "Everyone's the hero of their story. That's what Ms. Evans said in English."

"No," Poppy said, her low voice very fierce. "There's people who do things and people who never do—who say they will someday, but they just don't. I want to go on a quest. I've always wanted to go on a quest. And now that I have one, I'm not backing down from it. I'm not going home until it's complete."

Zach thought she might be right. He thought of his dad, who wanted to do things and then didn't. And he decided that even if it was dumb, he wanted to be the kind of person who was interesting enough to have a ghost talk to him. Even if the idea of the Queen being made of bones and filled with human ash grew more frightening the farther they got from home.

Alice laughed a little, uncomfortably, like what Poppy said about being a hero had hit a little close to home for her, too.

Leaving in the middle of the night and escaping from

the bus station already seemed like the kinds of things that happened on quests, so from that perspective they were doing really well. And thinking that made his tired brain slip into playing mode, which led to thinking like William.

"What if we *don't* go back right away?" he asked suddenly. "If we don't call anyone, we don't get in trouble, right? No one will know what happened. So if you take the bus back tonight—not the one to East Liverpool, the one back home—then your grandmother will never know anything. Or maybe we could even make it to East Liverpool and take the bus back from there. There's got to be a way for us to get there—we could walk if we have to. It can't be that many miles up the river. And the quest would be completed, despite some slight setbacks."

"In the dark?" Alice asked.

"We might as well try," Poppy said, brightening. "And you don't want to get in trouble, right?"

"I'm tired and it's the middle of the night," said Alice. "I don't feel like trying to follow some stupid map with a dying flashlight and the compass on my phone."

Zach thought about William the Blade, steering his ship by the North Star, and blinked up into the night sky. You were supposed to be able to find it by looking for the Big Dipper and then use that to find the Little Dipper. The North Star was the brightest of the Little

Dipper stars, and the one at the very end of the Little Dipper's handle.

That's the Polaris, he thought. *If we can see that, we can't get lost.*

"We'll find our way." When he spoke, he could feel William's voice creeping into his own voice, which was strange because William was gone. "And figure out a place to make camp."

"Make camp?" Poppy asked.

"Until break of day." Maybe it was exhaustion, but it wasn't that hard to think of what William would say. William always got into scrapes, so they didn't bother him. Heck, he liked trouble. "We'll eat the provisions we brought. Look, even according to the tiny map on the bus schedule, if we just follow the river, it should take us to East Liverpool. Our quest could still be completed."

"You want us to *walk?*" Alice said. "Both of you have gone crazy."

"My lady, I want us to *rest,*" Zach replied, offering her his arm. For once, he didn't feel uncertain. "I want us to take our meager supplies and turn them into a feast. I want us to make a fire and warm our bones. Then, in the morning, we can decide what to do from there. Should you, fair maid, wish to return home upon the morrow, then we shall entertain your arguments."

She laughed tiredly and looped her arm with his. "Fine. But I am going to want to go home upon the morrow, so plan on that happening."

"See, you missed the game." Poppy's mouth lifted in a triumphant smile. "You missed us playing. Admit it."

Zach stopped abruptly, whirling on her, the spell broken. "I told you not to talk about that, and *you said you wouldn't*." His voice came out harsher than he'd intended, almost a growl. Poppy took a step back.

"Okay," Alice said, grabbing his shoulder and propelling him down the alley. "So long as we're not freezing, I won't call home. If we can make camp, get warm, and sleep for a while, then let's do that and try not to get in more trouble than we're already in."

"Lady Jaye would be good at surviving on the streets," Poppy said innocently.

Zach glared.

"What? I was talking to Alice, not you. I'm allowed to talk to Alice about the game, aren't I? You didn't make any rules about that."

Alice sighed. "I don't even know what you two are fighting about. You both want to stay on this crazy adventure, and that's what we're doing."

"We should keep off big roads," Zach warned,

pointing toward a narrow street up ahead. "If someone sees us with the map and the flashlight, they're going to guess we're lost kids or runaways or something. We already had those people at the bus station after us."

"We still don't know if they were really chasing us," Poppy said. "Maybe they wanted to apologize about the crazy guy. Maybe they were afraid we were going to miss the bus. Or maybe they were aliens trying to take our faces."

Zach raised his eyebrows and started walking.

"Oh fine, yeah, let's use the dark scary road," Alice said, but she followed him anyway. "Let me see the map."

Poppy handed it over along with the flashlight. The asphalt of the alley was cracked, and they had to be careful not to stumble as they headed down it, passing heaped mounds of garbage and the back doors of restaurants.

There was a strange quiet in the air, as though everyone and everything was asleep. The echo of their footsteps was the loudest sound for several blocks. It felt both eerie and kind of exciting to Zach. It seemed to him that the whole world had become theirs for a little while.

"There's a stretch of woods," Alice said, waving the map. "Close to the water. We'd have to cross the highway to get there, but we're not too far."

"Is it a lot of woods?"

"Not really. But it's a park. Like a small, protected-area park looking out on the water, not a kid park with swings. Too small for a fire to be hidden, but probably big enough that we're not going to be seen from the road."

Zach nodded and let her direct them. He didn't know how to make a fire anyway. It had just seemed like something that you did when you made camp, along with making stews and playing lutes and swigging from jugs of cider.

"This was such a terrible idea," Alice muttered as they walked. "How did you convince me this was a good idea? This was a terrible, terrible, terrible idea."

They passed a supermarket with trucks pulled up to the back unloading flats of cardboard boxes. They passed a donut shop, closed, but with a light on inside. It gave off a warm waft of fresh dough and melting sugar. Zach's stomach growled, and he fished a Twizzler out of the pack. In comparison to the delicious smell, the candy tasted like sweet rubber.

He dug around and took out enough to give Alice and Poppy a couple of Twizzlers each, in case they were hungry too.

"Thank you, kind sir," said Poppy, with a little bow.

"I am not doing that with you," Zach said, biting the Twizzler savagely.

Poppy looked crestfallen, which was stupid because she'd been needling him a minute ago about playing. He didn't know why she was upset over something she started. If she hadn't pointed out that he was playing, he wouldn't have had to stop.

"Will you two quit it?" Alice said, aiming the beam of the flashlight at the sidewalk. She had the red candy hanging out of one side of her mouth and was chomping on it like it was a cartoon cigar.

Poppy looked at her feet. "We're cranky because we're tired, that's all."

Zach started to say something about how it was *her fault* that they were tired, when he realized saying that might actually prove her point that he was cranky.

The highway was a long stretch of lanes, with an even wider overpass, but at half past four in the morning, they saw only a single truck, headlights lighting up the street so brightly that it almost seemed like day. Once it zoomed by, Poppy and Alice held hands and raced for the median. They climbed the concrete block quickly; Zach's long legs made it easy for him to hop over. Then they ran across the lanes on the other side, even though there were no cars coming from either direction.

The edge of the woods was scrubby and sloped down at a steep angle. They tripped over sticks and uneven patches of earth. Long roping tendrils of bushes scraped at their legs. But after a few minutes of walking, Zach felt pretty hidden from the road. They could still see the lights of East Rochester on one side and could just glimpse the glimmering, rippling surface of the Ohio River stretching out on the other.

∾ CHAPTER EIGHT ∾

"WELL, THIS IS IT," ALICE SAID, SHADING THE FLASH-light with her hand. "You really think we can sleep out here?"

Even though they were close to the highway, the branches swinging overhead and the smell of leaf mold rising up from the forest floor made Zach feel a million miles away from the world he knew. Like maybe they really were in some fantasy land where dragons flew overhead and magic was possible.

Poppy sat down on the root of a tree. "Ugh, it's kind of damp and cold on my buttular region. We're going to need a hammock or something."

Zach knelt down. The ground was wet—the kind of wet that seeps up and soaks through clothes. He leaned against a tree, and despair washed over him. He liked the idea of an adventure—but what did he really know about having one? He wasn't used to roughing it. He wasn't used to bugs and dirt and all the stuff soldiers and pirates had to deal with. The only time he'd done anything even sort of like camping was when set he'd up his grandfather's old tent in his backyard; it had turned out to be full of spiders, and he'd ripped the old canvas trying to escape from them.

Pushing away from the tree, he unzipped his backpack and pulled out his sleeping bag. It was waterproof on one side, so if he opened it fully and spread it out like a picnic blanket, it would be big enough for all of them to sit on. *Maybe* keep them dry.

"That was smart, bringing that," Alice said, helping him to spread it out. "All I have is a change of clothes, toothpaste, and cookies that we got from Poppy's."

"You couldn't sneak back into your house," Poppy reminded her, crawling onto the sleeping bag, flopping down, and rooting around in her own pack. "And I didn't exactly give you advance notice."

Which, from Poppy, was almost an apology.

She took the Queen out of her bag. The doll's eyes were open, but as Poppy leaned her one way and then another, her eyes closed. Zach was glad to see that

Poppy had reattached the Queen's head, although it lolled slightly, like maybe Poppy had done it in a hurry and it wasn't on exactly right. The lolling head and closed eyes combined to make the Queen look as tired as they were, which was oddly reassuring. Poppy set the doll down and smoothed out her dress, then turned back to the bag. She tugged out a thin-looking coverlet, some safety pins and Band-Aids, a bar of chocolate that had gotten slightly mashed, a package of baby carrots, a bruised apple, a sweater, a pair of socks, a notebook, and one of her mermaid dolls.

"This is what I brought," she said. "To share, if you want any."

"We should take turns keeping watch," Zach said, "like we did on the bus." He took out his jar of peanut butter, package of crackers, oranges, and orange soda and put everything but the soda with the other supplies. Thirsty, he popped the tab on the drink. Fizzy foam bubbled up, and he quickly shifted the can over a mound of grass so the spraying liquid could spill onto the dirt. Then he took a long swig.

The bubbles hit the back of his throat in a satisfying way.

He thought about how he'd met them both, when they were all little kids. Poppy had been riding her bike up and down the block when she saw Zach sitting on his front steps, reading a beat-up old copy of *James and the Giant Peach*. She stopped to tell him that she'd read the book and it was good, but not as good as *The Witches*, and had he read *The Twits*? She was the one who'd met Alice, too, picking her up at a carnival, where they'd been the only two girls who had their faces painted like Batgirl instead of fairies and cats and clowns. The first time the three of them had hung out, they'd dangled upside down from the jungle gym until the blood rushed to their heads, trying to get their brains to work better so that they'd be able to move things with the combined power of their minds.

It seemed like such a long time ago.

"Watch? For what?" Alice said, reaching out her hand for the soda. "It's not like there are going to be marauding orcs or bears or wolves or creepy, crazy old bus riders. We're in a tiny strip of park."

"We'll sleep better if someone's on watch," said Zach, glancing at the doll's creepy, almost-sleeping face. He wanted someone making sure she didn't wake up and move around while their eyes were closed. "Or I will, anyway."

"I can stay up," Poppy said. "How about I wake one of you in an hour?"

"Not me," said Alice, yawning.

"I'll go second," Zach said. "Kick me if you get tired sooner."

She nodded. He finished off his orange soda in another two gulps. Alice had her enormous red coat off and was quickly layering her change of clothes—jeans and a blue hoodie with cat ears on the hood—on along with the gray dress she was wearing. Then she curled up like a bug under her coat, closed her eyes, and seemed to fall almost instantly into slumber.

Poppy had her thin blanket wrapped around her like a cape and was sitting with her back against the trunk of the tree, looking out at the water. Zach's eyes had adjusted enough to the moonlight that he could see the determined set of her jaw.

On her lap was the Queen, eyes open now as though she was on watch with Poppy, staring at nothing, the bone white of the doll's face seeming to glow in the gloom. Poppy's hand rested absently on the thing's chest, like she was holding it still. As Zach looked, his imagination fed him a horrible image: the Queen staggering across the uneven ground toward him, her chubby arms reaching for him. He wondered if he could convince Poppy to put the Queen back in her bag.

Poppy tilted her head, her gaze going to where he was sitting. "What?" she whispered.

He pointed to the doll, realizing he'd been staring. He kept his voice low. "This whole thing. Is it a game? Just tell me."

She narrowed her eyes. "It's real, Zach."

"Okay," he said, too tired to fight, lying down on the open sleeping bag and pillowing his head on one arm. "Wake me when it's my turn to be on watch."

She grunted a yes. He closed his eyes.

He dreamed about a big building near a river billowing smoke from its towers. And then, his dream vision swooping forward, he saw a yellow-haired girl watching as her father spun beautiful things from bone china. Teapots so thin and white that they seemed to glow from inside, covered in paper-fine china roses and lilies and leaves. Vases so fine that it seemed like a breath would shatter them, painted with dots of real gold.

Eleanor.

At the thought of her name, she seemed to turn toward him, her large black eyes widening like she was the one who saw a ghost.

His vision seemed smeared, and he was in front of a big, drafty house, welcoming a skinny and pinch-nosed woman. He knew, without knowing how, that he was looking at Eleanor's aunt and that she'd come down from the city to take care of Eleanor after Eleanor's mother had died six months past and it became clear that her father had no plans to remarry.

Children are dirty, her aunt said, and forbade her from playing outside. She gave her chores instead, making her wash the windows and sweep the floors and move the furniture around.

Children break things, her aunt said, and took away the dolls her father had made for her with spare clay, telling her they were too precious for her to keep.

The aunt displayed them, along with less successful bone china pieces Eleanor's father brought home from the factory. There was the bone china coffeepot wound with a vine that didn't curve quite right, resting on the sideboard in the dining room. There were sets of too-small teacups and a bowl with alligator feet that were too frightening and no one liked. There were countless vases marred by mistakes, that listed a little to one side or had gold paint that had smeared or blistered before they were fired or had three-dimensional flowers that had broken coming out of the kiln. Soon several mistakes rested on every side table, forcing Eleanor to tiptoe through the parlor to avoid breaking any.

Zach watched as Eleanor swept the floors, polished the silver, and hid things under her bed. Clothespins that she marked with ink so it seemed they had eyes. A pillowcase tied with string so it seemed like it had a neck and head. In the dark of her room at night, when her father and her aunt had gone to their beds, she took them out and played with them, whispering to herself, calling them by the same names as her old dolls.

Zach woke, blinking, to blue sky overhead, dotted with puffs of clouds.

Sunlight filtered through the canopy of green and brown leaves, dappling the ground with bright spots and shadow. He heard a sound that reminded him of the ocean. He'd gone to stay with his grandparents one summer, after his dad left, and they'd stayed in a house by the beach. He'd woken up with the crash of the waves in his head every morning.

But this wasn't the ocean, he knew, and a moment later he realized it wasn't the Ohio River, either. It was the sound of the highway, of cars and trucks whooshing past the woods, that sounded like breaking surf.

Zach sat up, blinking, stretching out his stiff limbs and looking around him. Alice was asleep on the sleeping bag, wrapped in her coat, braids falling in her face, a few pieces of white fuzz or feathers dusting her skin. Poppy was asleep too, her head lolling back against the tree. She'd fallen asleep on watch, Zach realized.

Turning, he saw the Queen resting in the dirt *right behind his head*, far from where she'd been the night before. Her black eyes were wide open, leering down at him. Now that it was daytime, he could see that the glass orbs were slightly too small for her eye sockets, leaving gaps in the corners. An ant crawled out from one of them, marching across her eye and up over her forehead into the thicket of her hair. Zach sprang up and scuttled away from her, his heart racing.

There was more of the white stuff settling on the grass. It looked almost like snow, but then he realized what he was looking at. It was the inside of the sleeping bag. Something had ripped it, cutting the fabric and pulling out the lining, and scattered that, along with all their food.

Baby carrots were tossed around in the dirt. The peanut butter was smeared on the bark of a nearby tree, the jar resting against a rock as if it had rolled there. Crackers were crumbled over the ground, and the chocolate bar was torn in half, pieces of gold foil scattered like confetti. He wondered who'd done this and then looked over at the doll's empty eyes, the ant on her bone-white cheek.

As he stared a squirrel ran up to the open jar of peanut butter and stuck its furry body inside.

Looking back at the night before, at Poppy and Alice waking him up in the middle of the night, the story about the Queen, the walk to the bus station, and making camp in the dark—all of those things felt distant, like they'd happened to someone in a book. It didn't seem possible that they'd spent the night in a tiny stretch of woods in a town he didn't know.

Turning back to where the doll rested, outside the circle of Poppy's arms, he wondered about other impossible things. Had a ghost really trashed their campsite? Was Eleanor watching him out of the Queen's glass eyes? A chill shivered up his spine.

Out in the middle of nowhere with an angry ghost and no idea how to get to her grave.

Oh yeah, they were in trouble.

✑ CHAPTER NINE ✑

ZACH WOKE ALICE BY SHAKING HER SHOULDER UNTIL she groaned and rolled over. Her braids spread out on the slashed sleeping bag and more white stuffing got caught in her hair.

"Five more minutes," she mumbled.

"Alice," he said quietly, poking her upper arm. "Something happened. Come on. Get up. You have to see this."

She opened her eyes and seemed surprised to see him there. "Where . . . ?"

"Stranded in East Rochester, Pennsylvania," Zach said with a shrug, hoping that gesture would somehow convey that he shared her feeling that everything had gotten pretty weird.

Then, as she took in the state of their campsite, she turned back to him with her brow furrowed in further puzzlement. "Who . . . ?"

He jerked his head toward Poppy and then the doll. "Do you believe in ghosts?" he asked, keeping his voice low. "Because I think I do now. For real and for sure."

"It could have been raccoons," Alice said. Her expression grew more horrified as she looked around. "I thought one of us was supposed to stay awake. Isn't that what you said last night?"

"Raccoons? Really?"

Alice nodded slowly, like maybe she wasn't so sure anymore. "Or Poppy did it. She was on watch."

"She's not *crazy*," Zach said. "And she'd have to be totally crazy to do this. Anyway, I thought you believed her about the ghost."

"I did. I do. I don't know. It was fun to play along." Alice pushed herself to her feet and walked around the woods, shivering. "This is too much. I don't believe *this*. Maybe animals ransacked the camp, or maybe Poppy was mad at us for wanting to go back and was trying to convince us to keep going. Either way, it wasn't a ghost."

"It seemed like an adventure last night, right?"

Zach said, but as he said it, he realized that it still did feel like an adventure—maybe even more than it had before—just not the same *kind* of adventure. He was scared. Little hairs were standing up along his arms, and he thought that maybe Alice was scared too. That was probably why she didn't want to believe in ghosts anymore.

But Zach wanted them to be real, wanted that desperately.

If they were real, then maybe the world was big enough to have magic in it. And if there was magic— even bad magic, and Zach knew it was more likely that there was bad magic than any good kind—then maybe not everyone had to have a story like his father's, a story like the kind all the adults he knew told, one about giving up and growing bitter. He might have been embarrassed to wish for magic back home, but there in the woods, it seemed possible. He looked over at the cruel, glassy eyes of the doll, so close that she could have touched his face.

Anything was better than no magic at all.

He thought about what Poppy had said—about how if they didn't go on the quest right then, they never would. How if they faltered, they'd never come back.

And he thought about his dream.

"I think it was Eleanor," Zach said. "Maybe her spirit's angry that we aren't taking this quest seriously enough. Maybe she's mad that we got off the bus before we got to the right stop. Or maybe she's mad that you want to go home."

"I'm sticking with the raccoon explanation," Alice said, picking up her coat and shouldering it on over her layers. "I bet Poppy got that story about Eleanor and the bones from one of her library books. I'm not trying to be mean. Poppy makes everything more interesting, but sometimes she gets carried away, you know?"

He thought about that, turning the words over in his mind. Alice was *saying* raccoons, but the rest of what she said pointed to Poppy. Poppy, who'd been the last one awake and who wanted to convince them both to stay on the quest. Who might have thought it was funny to put the Queen so close to him, knowing it would freak him out. "What about the ashes? Those were real."

Alice nodded, but not in a way that was agreeing. "I keep thinking about them. Maybe she took some ash from a grill and mixed in pieces of chicken bone. It was dark when we both looked at it. People fake that kind of thing onstage all the time."

He remembered that he'd wondered the same thing

the night before, about whether it was all a trick, but somewhere along the way he'd become convinced, and he didn't want to give that feeling up. He wanted to tell Alice about his dream and insist it meant that she was wrong, but he realized it didn't prove anything. He'd just dreamed about what Poppy described, like the way that after you see a movie, you sometimes dream yourself into it. He had no way to know if any of it was true or if it was just his brain regurgitating stuff.

Alice seemed to have lost interest anyway, unzipping the front part of Zach's backpack and sticking her hand inside, fishing around. "Do we have anything left? Any food?"

"No," he said. "I don't think so."

Her hand came out of his backpack, her fingers clutching a folded-up square of paper. She began to unfold it. "What's this?" she asked, distracted by her discovery. "A note? What's in here? Secret boy stuff?"

He knew exactly what she was holding.

"Give it to me," Zach said, grabbing for the paper.

Alice stood up, still reading, the smile sliding off her face. It was replaced with an expression of astonishment. Zach could see the scrawl of his own handwriting across the page and doodles decorating the margins. "These are the Questions Poppy gave you. You *answered* them. You told her you didn't, but you did."

"I guess I did. Can I have them back now?" He stood too, starting toward her. He lunged forward to grab the note from her hand.

She danced out of his way. "But why would you answer them when you were going to—?"

Alice never got to finish because at that moment Poppy jumped up from the sleeping bag with a shriek. She was crouching, blinking in the sunlight, her hands outstretched like she was ready to fight. It was a move of surprising awesomeness.

"Poppy?" Zach asked.

To his relief, Alice folded the note twice and shoved it into the pocket of her coat, then walked over to Poppy. They sat back down together. Zach could see that Poppy was still breathing hard.

"I dreamed that I was Eleanor. I fell—" Poppy said, pressing her hands against her face.

Zach didn't speak for a long moment. He wondered if he was a bad person if he didn't say anything about his dream. He wondered if Alice would think he was ridiculous if he did. The leaves overhead rustled. "I think you better look around," he said finally. "Did she seem angry? Because it looks like something trashed our camp."

Poppy stood up and dusted herself off, going over to the Queen and lifting her up. The doll's eyes moved to half-open, which made it appear as though she was watching them, the way his cat did when she was pretending to sleep.

"You think a ghost did this?" Poppy asked finally, turning back toward them.

"I don't," Alice said. "I think it was raccoons. But I thought that you'd say it was a ghost."

"It's classic poltergeist stuff, isn't it?" Zach asked.

"She's not a *poltergeist*," Poppy said, as though Zach had suggested her brand-new box set of *Doctor Who* DVDs were bootlegs. "And why would she toss out our food? Ruin the only thing we've got to sleep on? She wants us to take her to East Liverpool. She's not going to make it harder for us."

Zach thought he detected a note of uncertainty in her voice, though.

"Okay, whatever," he said. "You think it was raccoons too?"

Poppy looked around and sucked in her breath. "I don't know. What if it was Tinshoe Jones? What if he followed us?"

A shiver went up Zach's back, ending with a twitch between his shoulder blades. He could too easily imagine that weathered, smirking face watching them from the darkness. But there was no reason for Tinshoe to have gotten off the bus, followed them, waited for them to fall asleep, then tossed around their stuff. No reason at all. They didn't have anything he wanted. He probably thought they'd all been grabbed by aliens and gotten their faces stolen.

But Eleanor had plenty of reasons to be mad at Alice and was probably frustrated that she wasn't already in her grave.

"Look, I want to figure out what happened as much as you do," said Alice, looking between them like she wasn't sure which side she was on just then—maybe neither of theirs. "But can we please please get out of here first? The woods are creepy and I have to pee and I'm hungry."

"We passed that donut shop last night," Zach said.

Alice nodded. "Perfect. So long as they have a bathroom."

There wasn't much to pack up, so they didn't. The sleeping bag had been ruined along with the rest of their supplies, the long gashes making puffs of white stuffing well up with every gust of wind. The best they could do was gather up everything, roll up the wounded sleeping bag, and dump it all in one of the trash cans along the river.

No one else was there, but that didn't mean that no one else had been.

They walked back along the highway and managed to find a spot to cross that was less crazy than jumping over the median. Then they walked quietly, heads bent against the chill air. Zach could smell the melting sugar and rising dough of the shop blocks before he could see it. By the time he got to the door, he was practically drooling.

"How much money do we all have?" Poppy asked.

"I've got fifteen dollars and fifty cents." Zach had started with twenty-three dollars, but the bus ticket had cost him seven fifty and it would be another seven fifty to get back. Of the fifteen fifty he had, that left him with only eight dollars he could actually spend.

"I have twenty," said Alice.

"Eleven and a bunch of pennies," said Poppy. "We should save something for later. For lunch and the trip back."

But as they opened the door, Zach's stomach growled, and saving money was the last thing on his mind. There were rows and rows of baskets along the back wall, each of them filled with a different flavor of donut, their frostings bright under the lights. There were cinnamon cider donuts, Boston cream and jelly crullers, chocolate sprinkle, rainbow sprinkle, maple cream, sour cream, old-fashioned, blueberry, toasted coconut, bear claws, and apple fritters. And then beneath the glass of the counter, stranger flavors—Froot Loops, peanut butter, ketchup, pickle juice, mandarin orange, honeycomb, lox and cream cheese, lobster, cheeseburger, fried chicken, wasabi, acorn flour, bubblegum, Pop Rocks, and spelt.

The man behind the counter had a thick, wild head of black hair. It stuck up as though he'd been electrocuted, except where it crawled down his cheeks into sideburns. "Get you kids something?" he asked as the bell on the door rang. "The wasabi donuts just came out of the fryer. They're still hot."

They were also a muted green color and smelled spicy, like hot peppers.

"Uh," Zach said, glancing at the menu. "Can I have a hot chocolate? A big one."

He took his warm cup with its spirals of whipped cream to one of the small plastic tables. Alice headed to the bathroom in the back while Poppy ordered two more hot chocolates. They sat for a while, letting the heat of the paper cups warm their fingers.

Then they each ordered a donut. Zach got Pop Rocks, Alice got maple cream, and Poppy got Froot Loops. The crumbling cake was delicious, and there were real Pop Rocks inside that fizzed against Zach's tongue. He licked his fingers when he was done, forgetting that he hadn't washed his hands in a very long time.

The hot chocolates had been two fifty a piece and the donuts were a dollar twenty-five, costing them each three seventy-five and leaving Zach with four twenty-five that he could spend for the whole rest of the trip. Poppy had even less. He hoped she had at least twenty-five pennies, or she wasn't going to be able to pay her bus fare home.

Poppy sat the Queen on a nearby chair. The doll slumped, her head twisted on an angle, her hair rumpled as though she'd really been sleeping on it. Her half-closed eyes were bright with reflected light.

"If you died," Poppy said, keeping her voice low. "Do you think you'd want to be a ghost?"

"If I was murdered, then yeah, definitely," Zach said. "So I could haunt my killer and get revenge."

"Get revenge by doing what?" Alice asked, laughing. "You would be a disembodied spirit. What are you going to do? Yell 'boo!' at them? Try to convince them to go on a stupid road trip?"

"I could throw stuff around," Zach reminded her.

"Maybe," Alice said. "I'd do it if I could be me, but see-through. The whole world would be like my television. I could visit the people I loved. But not if I had to repeat the same thing over and over again, like haunting some stretch of road or going up and down stairs."

"Even if you couldn't talk to anyone?" Zach asked.

Alice looked briefly uncomfortable. "I'd definitely want there to be a ghost society with ghost friends."

Poppy pushed her hair back. "Well, what if you decided you wanted to come back from the dead and then changed your mind, but you were stuck?"

"You mean like how I'm stuck here in East Rochester?" said Alice, and then she took a big swallow of hot
chocolate.

Zach thought he'd better interrupt that line of conversation. "Would you want to be a ghost, Poppy?"

She shrugged. "I don't know. Lingering around,
whooshing past people who'd never see me? It's scary
to imagine things happening and me not being able to
affect them. I keep thinking about the dream I had. It
was like I was really her—I was climbing around on the
slate tiles of the roof of this giant house, trying to keep
away from the windows while I waited for my father to
get home. I had something really important to tell him.
Up there, I could see for what seemed to be miles—I
could see the river and boats and the iceman's truck in
front of a house down the street—but I kept slipping
and catching myself on the copper gutters. And I heard
this woman's voice from behind me, whispering to me,
telling me I better get inside or she was going to make
me sorry. She had a broom, and she was sticking it out
the window, trying to hit me."

Zach thought about his own dream of the pinch-
faced woman and the big Victorian house of flawed
pottery. He wanted to tell her about the dream, but
he felt a little silly about it. When he'd woken, it had

seemed so obvious that the dream was real, that it had been given to him by their ghost. But now, in the warmth of the donut shop, after Alice being so certain there was no ghost, he was unsure about everything.

"Do you think that was really what happened?" Poppy asked, leaning forward eagerly like there was only one possible right answer. "Do you think she's trying to tell us about her death? Imagine that the whole time she was in the cabinet, she was just waiting for one of us to take her out."

Zach opened his mouth to describe his dream, but it seemed as though not telling Poppy and Alice what had happened to his action figures or why he didn't want to play made it hard to tell about other things too. It felt like everything was all mixed up together, weighing down his tongue.

The man moved behind the counter, dumping a fresh batch of peach muffins into a tissue-lined bin. "No problem," he called to them.

"What?" Zach asked, confused.

"Your blond friend sounds pretty hungry," he said, coming out from behind the counter with a pink-glazed donut on a paper plate. He placed it down in front of the doll. "Here. On the house. It's Pepto-Bismol flavored. We're trying it out to see if it gets on the regular menu."

As the man walked back into the kitchen, Zach could only stare after him. "Did he—?" Zach whispered.

"It was just a joke," Alice said quickly, but she looked nervous. "You know, because we had a doll. He was pretending it was real."

"Why would he do that?" Poppy asked.

"Because he thinks he's being some kind of cool adult." Alice took another sip of her hot chocolate and then pushed it away like it had burnt her. She shuddered. Zach thought uncomfortably about what Leo had said on the walk home from school way back when. *Somebody walk over your grave?*

Your blond friend. There was something familiar about the words, though, something that snagged in Zach's mind. "No, wait. Tinshoe. That's what he said on the bus—'I'm not going to talk to the blonde.' Because he didn't like the way she was looking at him. Remember?"

"I remember that," said Alice. Poppy nodded.

"Do you think he was talking about the doll too?" Zach felt cold, and the food he'd eaten churned in his stomach. He'd wanted the ghost to be real, but the more real Eleanor seemed, the more scared he was. He tried not to look over at the Queen. He tried not to think about what it meant that she sounded hungry.

He tried not to notice that her cheeks seemed a little rosier today, like she was feeding on something other than donuts.

They had to bury her, and they had to bury her soon.

"Okay, well . . . ," Alice said. She checked the face of her cell phone, then took out the map. It was ripped down the middle, but she rested it on the table so all the streets lined up. "It's ten forty-three now, and the next bus isn't until four thirty. There's time and all, but I really have to be on that bus."

"East Liverpool isn't that far," said Poppy. "Zach said so last night. We could still make it. On foot. Like real adventurers."

They were all quiet for a long moment.

"I'm going," Poppy said, picking up the doll and cradling it in her lap. Her cheek rested against its pale bone china brow. Its eyes seemed more open than before. Pale milk glass with a black center. "With or without you guys." Her voice was small, though.

Zach thought about all the food thrown around the woods, about the slashed sleeping bag. And he wondered what else a ghost could do.

Have you ever heard this one? When you drive past a cemetery, you have to hold your breath. If you don't, the spirits of the newly dead can get in your body through your mouth and possess you.

But he'd already decided. He wasn't turning back. "I'm still up for an adventure," he said with a nod. "I'm in."

Alice slapped her hands down on the table like she was calling a meeting to order. "I'm not a coward. I care about adventures too, okay? It's not that. But I need to get home by tonight or my grandmother is going to lose her mind. She's going to call the cops. She'll make sure I don't go anywhere for months, and she'll remind me of what I did whenever I ask for permission to do anything for the rest of my life. Forever. So I am not going to be late. Okay?" Her voice got louder, and the words came out faster as she spoke, and when she finished there was a long silence.

"Okay," Poppy said finally.

"So, look, I want to go, but I want you to promise we'll get back home *today*. The bus leaves here at four thirty, and I want you to promise we're not going to miss it. Promise that we'll turn around in time if we have to. Promise me that you'll get on it with me."

"But what if we're almost there and—" Poppy started.

"No way," Alice said. "We still have to get to the graveyard and bury the Queen and find the bus station before the bus from East Liverpool leaves—at three forty-five. If we make it to East Liverpool and there's time, great, but remember that the bus leaves earlier from there. I'll come with you, but if it doesn't look like we'll make it, we all come back together."

Poppy looked reluctant. "I'm not going back without finishing this quest."

"Then I'm going to the bus station now," Alice said, pushing back her chair and standing. "You and Zach can adventure by yourselves. I'm not going with you."

"Wait," Zach said, standing too and reaching for her. "We started this together. We need to stay together. We can make it to East Liverpool and still get home."

Alice folded her arms over her chest.

"Poppy," Zach said.

She sighed. "Fine. But if we're going to make it by Alice's deadline, we have to go now. And we have to go fast."

Zach put out his hand to pull Poppy to her feet. "We're already up. We're waiting on you."

Poppy stood without letting him help, holding the Queen under her arm. "You believe me now, don't you? About the dream. About the ghost. You believe me, right?"

Zach opened his mouth to tell her that he'd dreamed

about Eleanor too. But just then, Alice said, "Sure we do," and the moment passed.

Instead he picked up the Pepto-Bismol donut and bit into it.

The frosting was sickly sweet, but it was the bitter taste underneath that stayed on his tongue.

☙ CHAPTER TEN ❧

ADVENTURING TURNED OUT TO BE BORING. ZACH thought back to all the fantasy books he'd read where a team of questers traveled overland, and realized a few things. First he'd pictured himself with a loyal steed that would have done most of the walking, so he hadn't anticipated the blister forming on his left heel or the tiny pebble that seemed to have worked its way under his sock, so that even when he stripped off his sneaker he couldn't find it.

He hadn't thought about how hot the sun would be either. When he put together his bunch of provisions, he never thought about bringing sunblock. Aragorn never wore sunblock. Taran never wore sunblock. Percy never wore sunblock. But despite all that precedent for going without, he was pretty sure his nose would be lobster-red the next time he looked in the mirror.

He was thirsty, too, something that happened a lot in books, but his dry throat bothered him more than it had ever seemed to bother any character.

And, unlike in books where random brigands and monsters jumped out just when things got unbearably dull, there was nothing to fight except for clouds of gnats, several of which Zach was pretty sure he'd accidentally swallowed.

Also, it wasn't like they were walking through the awesome vistas of Middle Earth—a forest full of Ents or elves, a mountain pass brimming with orcs and ice—they were mostly walking past industrial buildings and a bowling alley. Eventually the warehouses thinned out until it was just highway on one side and water on the other. They kept heading along the road, pausing occasionally to kick rocks or adjust their backpacks.

Alice was walking ahead, with Zach behind her. She had a blade of grass and was trying to turn it into a whistle, a trick she claimed her uncle could do. So far all she'd managed was to make a lot of spitting noises.

"I had an idea," Poppy said, speeding her pace to draw even with Zach. She was still carrying the Queen, the doll settled against her hip like it was a child. He tried to keep his gaze from going to it. "About William. About who his father is."

"You promised not to talk about the game." He was tempted to, though. He wanted to know how the story would have ended, since he'd never get to play it. And he was bored.

"No," Poppy said with a trickster's smile. "I agreed not to ask why you stopped playing. And I didn't."

Zach sighed. He was arguing because he thought he should, not because his heart was really in it. "I guess I had some ideas too," he admitted.

Poppy looked at him with astonishment. "You did?"

"He's my character, after all. But even if his father is the king of the whole Gray Country, he's going to stay a pirate. He's happy where he is, on the *Neptune's Pearl*. No dad is going to change that."

Poppy was looking at him oddly, like she wanted desperately to ask why he thought about any of this stuff, since he'd said he didn't want to play anymore. But for once, she was smart and didn't. "Even if his father was the Duke of Deepwinter Barrow?"

They didn't have a doll to represent him, but the Duke was a bad guy, through and through. They'd loved making up his crimes. He'd been raising a zombie army of broken dolls to march over the rest of the lands. He'd chopped off the heads of his enemies and abducted an evil priestess to be his duchess. Another action figure that Zach used to play had fought them over by the Silver Hills and nearly died. He was being healed by one of Alice's dolls, in a temple she'd made from a shoe box.

"That would be pretty good," Zach said. "If William was the Duke's son, then he could get close enough to assassinate him. Or maybe he could *say* that he was the Duke's son—maybe he's really someone else's kid entirely. Maybe someone even better. Like an ancient pirate lord or some kind of monster."

Poppy looked flustered. She was good at making up stories, but she wasn't always good at accepting the stuff he and Alice made up, no matter how awesome it was. It took her a little while to accept a universe she didn't have total control over.

Alice halted abruptly.

The path had ended. Up ahead, another big fat river flowed into the Ohio, making it impossible to go farther. Two bridges spanned the river, but he could see that they were useless to three kids on foot. One was a railway bridge, rusted and abandoned, with large gaps where metal rails had fallen off. The other was a massive concrete three-lane highway, with a toll booth on one side and no room for walking on the shoulder.

"Well, that's that," Alice said. She had a strange expression on her face, half relief and half disappointment.

Zach sighed, gazing up along the waterway. There were shabby-looking marinas on either side of the big unknown river. If this was a book or a movie, they would meet a mysterious figure with a boat and that person would ferry them across. Like Charon. Probably try to trick them too—but if they were clever, they could make it. And if he was William, he wouldn't need to be ferried across because he'd have the *Neptune's Pearl*—his two-masted schooner—and all his crew.

But in real life, those things didn't matter. He was suddenly aware of how tired he was.

"Let's go ask," Poppy said. "Maybe there's a ferry?"

It was only a little after noon, so they walked down to the marina. The few buildings—an oversize boat storage area, a lean-to, and an office—sat beside three long docks, with an array of boats separated by berms. Two little kids were leaning over the side of a piling with a fishing net, watching something in the water.

"You want to split up?" Zach asked. "See if we can find somebody who might know how to cross?"

"Okay," said Alice, glancing toward the office. "Let's meet back here in five minutes."

"I'm going to talk to those kids," Poppy said, turning to head in their direction.

He walked a little ways, inhaling the smell of diesel and river and tar baking in the sun. The day had turned warm, and Zach wondered if it would be possible to swim across. He wondered if Alice had had the right idea, going into the main building. There was probably air-conditioning and maybe even a water fountain up there.

As he wandered he spotted an old rowboat, pulled up to one side of the dry dock and leaned against some pilings. The paint was chipped along the sides, and he didn't see any oars, but for a moment, he imagined them ferrying themselves across. As he got closer, though, he saw the hull had enough rot damage to keep it from being seaworthy. He didn't need to know much about boats to know it would leak like crazy if he put it in the water.

With a sigh, he studied the sleek motorboats, shaped like long cigars, and the towering, multilevel fishing vessels with tall antennae shooting off of them like whiskers on a cat. He couldn't imagine the sort of people who owned boats like that, but he was pretty sure that they didn't give kids rides just for asking.

Despite reading tons about pirates and drawing the *Neptune's Pearl* in such detail that he'd figured out most of the rigging, and even building model ships, Zach had never been on a boat.

He took another look at the rowboat and wondered if it might be possible to patch it. Maybe he could find some nails and wood glue and tar. And if that didn't work, then maybe they could bail water faster than the boat could sink?

"Zach!"

He turned at the sound of his name being shouted. Poppy was standing next to the two kids with the net and waving him over.

"Brian's dad is trying to sell a dinghy," she said when Zach stepped onto the dock. It dipped underneath him and he steadied himself, lamenting his lack of sea legs.

"Uh-huh," he said warily. They had maybe fifteen dollars before they were dipping into the funds for the way back. "How much does he want for it?"

"Twenty-five." Poppy glanced at Zach's watch and raised her eyebrows. "But Brian said that maybe we could trade if we had anything he wanted. And he'll throw in oars."

"There's no other way across?"

She shook her head, making her red hair fly around

her. The sun had pinked her nose and deepened her freckles. "There's another bridge, but it's more than a mile away. If we're on the water, Brian says we can make it to East Liverpool in a half hour. Easy."

Brian nodded. "We go up that way to fish sometimes. It's not far," the other kid said.

"Okay," Zach said. "Let's see this thing."

Brian led them down to the end of the dock, where a few small dinghies and rowboats were moored. Three rowboats rocked gently beside one another, buffered by plastic fenders. Brian pointed to the one on the end, painted a slate gray. It was beat-up, but afloat, with no visible leaks. A lot better than the rotted-out one Zach had found near the dry dock.

"Can you give us a second to talk it over?" Zach asked.

Brian shrugged and headed back to where his friend was manning the net, trailing it through the water like he was going to catch something by sheer accident. As Zach watched the kid go he saw Alice crossing the gravel-covered yard toward them.

It was interesting watching her when she didn't notice herself being observed. Her coat was tied around her waist. She looked determined and sweaty and a little bit hopeful. Her angular face and thin eyebrows were utterly familiar, but he realized for the first time that she looked like one of those older, mysterious girls he wondered at sometimes in the mall, and that made her strange to him.

"All I've got is a necklace," Poppy said, touching the thin silver chain around her neck protectively. She wore a tiny typewriter key charm on it. He hadn't seen her without it since she'd gotten it from her father on her birthday. "I'll trade that, though."

"I've got my watch and a flashlight," Zach said. "And a book I'm pretty sure they don't want."

Alice walked up to them, pushing back her braids impatiently. "Hey, look, guys, I talked to an old guy up at the marina office. He said there was *no way* to walk to East Liverpool. I know you're going to be mad, but he said it was *impossible*, Poppy." She sighed. "I'm sorry."

"What if we don't go by foot?" Poppy said, pointing to the gray boat.

"Do we even know which way the current of the river runs?" Alice asked. "Or anything about boats?"

Poppy looked momentarily thrown, then she frowned. "What's to know? We just row harder if the current is against us."

Zach itched to be on the water, even in the little dinghy.

"You promised we'd go back," Alice said. "Both of you said that if we couldn't get to East Liverpool in time to get the bus, we'd go back to East Rochester. Well, it's time to turn around."

Poppy hesitated, and Zach stayed silent far too long.

"Seriously?" Alice asked them. "You're really going to break your promises?"

"It's not that," Zach said, looking longingly at the water. "It's just that I think we can still make it."

Alice's expression hardened into a tight, unfriendly smile. Her eyes shone like chips of glass. "Oh no, you have to come back with me," she told Zach. "Even if Poppy doesn't come with us."

"Yeah?" he said, trying to sound like he didn't care—like he didn't even know what she was going to threaten him with. He did know, though, and he did care.

"I'll tell her," Alice said. "That you lied, and what you lied about."

"Tell me?" Poppy asked. "Wait, what do you mean? Tell me what?"

"Nothing," Zach said, stepping back from them. He took a deep breath of diesel and river muck. He couldn't think—all he knew was that if Poppy found

out about the Questions, she would never stop picking at his reasons for lying about them until the whole
story came out. Imagining that filled him with nameless
panic. "Alice is right about us promising. If she wants to
go back, then—"

Poppy interrupted him, looking at Zach like if she
stared hard enough, she could read his mind. "What
don't you want me to find out?"

He remembered, too late, how much Poppy hated
her friends keeping secrets from her.

"It's *nothing*," Zach insisted.

"Then tell me," Poppy said. She hesitated a moment,
then looked at Alice. *"Tell me."*

"Come on," Alice said. "Give up. The game's over.
We're going back. Let's all just go back. It was still fun.
It was still a quest."

"No way," said Poppy. "I could tell Zach something
that I bet you don't want him to know, *Alice*. I know a
secret too."

Alice's whole face changed. He wondered if he'd
been so transparent, if it had been as clear when he'd
figured out just what he had to lose. And he understood,
right then, why Poppy was so upset about Zach and
Alice not telling Poppy things. Because whatever Alice
didn't want Poppy to say had to be pretty bad. Maybe

Alice had talked about how much she hated him or said that he smelled or how stupid he was. Maybe she had made fun of him to Poppy, snickering behind his back.

"You wouldn't do that," Alice said, her voice hushed. "You're my best friend. That's a secret."

"Just *tell me*," Zach said. "Come on. Whatever it is, I won't be mad. At least I don't think I'll be mad."

Poppy laughed, and Zach thought he saw a strange dancing light in the glass eyes of the doll, as though the Queen was laughing too. When Poppy spoke, her voice was different. She could be mean sometimes, but never before did she seem gleeful about being cruel. "She's not going to tell you. I win at blackmail. Alice has to come, and since *you* apparently have to do what *she* wants, you have to come too. So come on, let's buy this boat."

"You don't understand how much trouble I'm going to get in," Alice said, running her fingers through her braids.

"I don't care. You didn't care about me, and now I don't care about you either," said Poppy.

"But you promised!" Alice said, her voice anguished.

"*I don't care,*" Poppy repeated.

Zach paced down the dock, too angry at everyone to be ready to give in to anyone, especially those kids with their fishing net who were going to try and talk him out of all the cash they had. He glanced at Alice, who was staring at the water in an agony of indecision. And he looked back at the three rowboats and the dinghy, which, now, under his resentful gaze, looked increasingly shabby.

None of it was right. This wasn't how their quest was supposed to go.

He had read lots of stories where heroes succeeded in spite of long odds, where they accomplished a task that everyone else had failed at. He wondered for the first time about all the people who'd gone before those heroes, about whether they'd been heroic too or whether they'd been at each other's throats, before everything had gone wrong. He wondered if there was a point where they realized they weren't going to make it, weren't going to beat those long odds—that in the legend that would follow, they were going to be the nameless people that failed.

At the very end of the dock, Zach stopped. He drew in his breath.

In front of him was a tiny sailboat, low and slim, only a little bigger than the dinghy, but made from fiberglass. A black-and-white striped sail was folded loosely around the boom, the symbol of a sunfish visible on the Dacron cloth. Someone must have just left it, intending to come right back, because the centerboard was pulled out and there were two life jackets piled together in the cockpit.

Across the stern was one word in a curling script: PEARL.

Zach jumped down onto the hull, his sneakers hitting the curved deck. The boat rocked wildly underneath him, and he had to pinwheel his arms and grab the mast to steady himself. With a grin breaking across his face, he looked up at Alice and Poppy.

"We're not buying anything," he said. "We're pirates, remember?"

Their twin expressions of disbelief only made his smile wider.

∽ CHAPTER ELEVEN ∾

POPPY NEARLY CAPSIZED THE BOAT GETTING INTO IT. Zach sat in the center, fingers splayed against the hull, with his legs in the shallow cockpit as she climbed down rungs drilled into one of the pilings. First she handed him her backpack, which he dumped next to his, in a small cavity under the centerboard. The boat rocked lightly. When her foot touched the edge of the deck, though, it tipped dangerously toward her. Zach threw his weight hard to the other side, hoping to balance it out. Poppy staggered, falling on her knees with a yelp. After a few moments of wobbling, the boat settled.

"Wow," she said, trailing her fingers through the water and lifting them up, like it was marvelous to be so close to the river and not swimming in it. "We're actually doing this thing."

"You're next," Zach called up to Alice. "If Poppy goes to the prow and I stay in the center, it won't be as hard for you to come aboard. At least I think it won't be hard."

"Let me cast off the lines first," Alice said, beginning to untie the boat from the pilings.

"I don't know if that's such a good idea," Zach said. "We can untie them from here and leave the ropes."

Zach tried to remember everything he'd ever read about sailing, which was a lot. The prow was the point of the boat and the aft was the back end—he was pretty sure about that. And the stern was another word for the back end. The mast was the big thing sticking up from the center of the boat. Starboard was to the right and port was to the left. The boom was the other metal part that the sail attached to, making the L shape that swung the sail where it was supposed to be to catch the wind. And the rudder was the part that you steered with. But that was just vocabulary, and none of it would help him at all if he couldn't recall the principles.

Alice put her hand on her hip. "What if we have to dock in East Liverpool? We can't dock without rope."

He couldn't argue with that, but he could worry as the boat, no longer held by a line at its bow, began to angle more sharply in its berth. Then Alice untied the aft line. At first the *Pearl* swung closer to the piling, one of the boat's fenders bumping against the floats holding up the dock. But while Alice scampered down the piling, the *Pearl* began to drift away from the dock.

In books, Zach remembered, there was some kind of pole that you used to cast off, hooking on to the dock to hold the boat in place once the ropes were released, and pushing off with the pole when everyone was on. He didn't have anything like that. He scrambled to grab hold of a piling, but it was too late.

"Jump!" Zach yelled to Alice. "Now!"

And she did. She pushed herself off the piling and half fell into the cockpit, making Zach have to crouch low to keep his balance. The boat sat lower in the river with a third person weighing it down, water sloshing up over the edges of the hull, but it didn't tip over. As Zach pushed off the far piling that marked the outer edge of the berth, he realized that they'd done it. They were moving. They'd pirated a boat.

For better or for worse, they were on Beaver River, the current swinging them toward the Ohio. The wind overhead gusted with the promise of good sailing.

And despite the fact that Alice hadn't even wanted to come, she was laughing.

Sailing was supposed to be simple, so long as the wind was right behind you. You just let out the sail—Zach remembered that term and that it involved letting the sail billow, which must be done with one of the three ropes attached to the deck, although he wasn't exactly sure which one—and the sail filled with lots of air, which propelled the boat straight forward.

But if the wind was coming from the side—which it usually was—then things were harder. You still caught the wind, but because of the keel on the bottom of the boat, instead of just moving away from where the wind was blowing, you mostly went straight. Mostly.

At least that was how all the books said it was supposed to work. But reading about it and doing it were completely different. He understood the theory, the ropes, the figuring out the wind, and the positioning yourself on the boat, but he couldn't seem to make the Sunfish actually sail. They sat in the water, pushed around by the current, spinning slowly.

Poppy was strapping herself into one of the life vests, while Zach flailed around, overwhelmed, pretending to know what he was doing, pulling on ropes and testing things out. She offered the other vest to Alice, who took it grudgingly. Although Alice seemed to have accepted that they were continuing on the quest, she clearly hadn't come close to forgiving Poppy. It was a very tiny boat, but Alice managed to sit as far from Poppy as was possible.

Zach wanted to say something to them, to make them talk to each other, but it was hard to concentrate on that while he was pulling on lines to lift the sail. They were coming up on the two bridges. The first one was high enough not to present much of a problem, but the second had more pylons underneath it, and Zach wanted to be sure they steered wide of those.

He suddenly remembered that he hadn't dropped the rudder. Crawling to the stern of the boat, he pushed it down and grabbed the tiller so he could start to steer. Alice started working on the sail. It billowed wildly, flapping back and forth, the boom swinging to the right.

Starboard, some part of his brain reminded him.

"Tighten it," he yelled, and she did, pulling the rope until the wrinkles went out of the sail. And suddenly they were moving. Spray splashed up off the water and wet their hair and faces like raindrops. Wind ruffled Zach's hair.

Despite the fear of Poppy finding out about the Questions and the weirdness of Poppy and Alice having some secret, in that moment he felt pretty happy. He loved the feeling of the river beneath them and ahead of them and behind them. He was the *captain* of a real ship, a real ship really called the *Pearl*. It was almost too much magic to bear, but for once he didn't question it. He threw back his head and grinned up into the blue of the sky.

On either side the banks were green, occasionally punctuated with oil tanks and industrial buildings and a few stretches of houses. Alice let out the sail more, and the boat sped, tilting starboard, the port side rising up and making them lean against it with their feet balanced against the edge of the cockpit, trying to flatten things out. They were cutting through the water, faster and faster.

"We're going to flip!" Poppy yelled.

"Hold on," said Alice.

Zach pushed the tiller so that they moved to the left, and they slowed a little, flattening. The sail began to luff, flapping noisily, and Alice tightened it to their new, slower speed. That had been exhilarating but also scary.

Poppy scrambled into the cockpit and got the Queen from her pack, zipping the doll beneath her hoodie. "In case we flip," she said. "I'm afraid of her going overboard."

"Don't you think she'd be safer where she was?" Zach asked.

"Obviously, I don't," Poppy told him.

Alice raised both her eyebrows, as if to remind Zach that Poppy was crazy.

It took a while to get used to what made the boat move faster, when to let out the sail or tighten it, what to do when the wind changed slightly (which it seemed to do every ten minutes), and how to stay out of the way of other boats.

They sailed for what seemed like hours, but was really only a single hour. Usually when Zach was doing something, even walking, he could kind of zone out and think about other things. But handling the boat was like playing basketball—it demanded every bit of his attention. Maybe if he'd been more experienced at it, things would have been different, but half the time he was terrified that the boat was going to topple over because it was zooming along at such a steep angle. The other half of the time, the sail hung slack, and he barely could get it to move.

Occasionally, a massive barge would pass by, sending a wake that forced them to grip on to anything they could as the sailboat careened from side to side, nearly throwing them off like a bull at a rodeo.

"Do you think the *Pearl*'s owner has noticed their boat's gone?" Poppy asked as they passed a rocky island rising up on the right-hand curve of the river. A few scrub trees grew on it.

Zach shifted uncomfortably. When he'd played William the Blade robbing people, he was always able to find a good excuse—mostly that that were bad guys—but in real life, excuses felt different. "When we dock in East Liverpool, we'll call the marina and tell them where the *Pearl* is. The owners will be able to pick up the boat, so hopefully they won't worry for too long."

Alice pointed to the island, clearly not listening to Zach and Poppy. "It seems like anything could be there, doesn't it? I bet no one has ever stepped foot on the shore. Imagine if there was a gateway next to one of those rocks and no one knew it because everything that goes there disappears."

Zach looked at the island as they sailed past, imagining.

Around the curve was an industrialized stretch of river with houses along the eastern shore and pipes, tanks, and barges along the other. Many were docked, and a few powerboats raced between them, making the water choppy. The constant rocking of the boat made it hard to steer. Zach's muscles were sore from leaning hard in one direction, and his clothes were soaked through with spray.

Alice checked her phone.

"What time is it?" Zach asked her.

"About two forty," she said. "We've got an hour to get there and find the bus station."

Poppy looked over nervously. Even though this had started out as her plan, Zach thought that she looked as worried as the rest of them.

"This is taking longer than we thought," Poppy said finally. "Longer than those boys said."

Zach was tempted to point out that it would have taken a lot longer if they were rowing, but he didn't. Even though they didn't have much time, he was still feeling pleased. He and Alice had gotten good at sailing the little boat. They were going faster, catching the wind and skimming through the water like a bike speeding downhill.

Zach leaned back and watched the shoreline, watched the woods turn to town and highway and then back to woods again, watched the few houses built close enough to the river that he could spot them. In other places, houses on the river would have been big estates with their own private docks and vast lawns, but here were regular houses, like it was no big deal to live on the water.

Then they passed more industrial buildings, these a lot older-looking, with crumbling chimneys reaching into the sky. The city beyond them reminded him a little of a more sprawling version of his town—a couple of nice Victorian houses with boarded-up windows and a sluggish central square. There was a small metal bridge, which the boat was about to pass beneath. He could hear the rattle of cars across its metal supports. Up ahead, the river curved south.

"Wait," Poppy said, pointing back at the town they'd just passed. "You've got to turn around. That's East Liverpool. That's the old pottery factory. Look."

Zach half stood, he was so surprised. "Turn around? Do you understand that the current is running the way we've been sailing? And the wind—if we turn about, we're going against the wind."

"But we've got to go back." Poppy's eyes were wide. "We missed it."

He looked at Alice and he could see the blank terror in her face. She had no more idea how to turn a sailboat around than he did.

"Okay," he said. "So you swing the boom, and I'll pull the tiller."

Alice nodded. Zach steered toward the sandy bank to give them plenty of room to come about. "When the sail shifts, we're going to have to change sides too," he told Poppy. "So get ready."

He pulled on the tiller, and Alice pulled in the rope so that the sail tightened and swung. The boat turned in a single graceful movement, and then, with the wind and the current coming at them the wrong way and almost no idea what they were doing, the boat listed to one side and went over, dumping them all into the river.

The water was shockingly cold, and the impact of it rattled him down to his bones. He grabbed for the side of the boat.

Alice sputtered to the surface. Poppy was treading water, holding on to the mast and the sail.

Zach swam to the keel, which rose from the hull like a shark's fin. "Get clear for a second."

Poppy kicked away from the boat, dog-paddling toward Alice.

Zach threw his weight against the hull, and it righted itself, its sail lifting up off the water. He scrabbled to pull himself on board.

Alice heaved herself onto the deck, and then both of them grabbed for Poppy, who kept one arm pressed across her chest to hold the doll in place even as she was hauled onto the boat. Another barge was passing to their left, creating a rippling wake that made their boat rock wildly again. And Zach could see that two barges followed it. For a moment they just drifted farther in the wrong direction, sail slack, holding on.

Alice lunged at Poppy. "This is enough. The end. Enough with the creepy doll and the lying and the trying to make this true." With those words, her hand darted out and snatched the doll from where it was half zipped inside Poppy's wet hoodie.

Poppy screeched, and Zach gasped, but it was too late. Alice threw it overhand, up and out toward the barge and the deep water.

Everything froze for a long moment. The Queen hit the waves with barely a splash, the water seeming to soak her dress in slow motion, drawing it down. Her hair spread in a golden wave, and her dull black eyes looked up at them as she bobbed for a moment before sinking in a froth of bubbles.

❧ CHAPTER TWELVE ❧

ZACH DIDN'T THINK ABOUT IT. HE DOVE.

When he was a little kid, his mom had taken him
to swimming classes at the YMCA. He remembered the
bleachy smell of the chlorine and the feel of the orange
swimmies inflated too tightly against his upper arms and
the way all the kids' shouting bounced off the ceiling to
echo. And he remembered how to kick like a frog.

He kicked now, over and over, toward the Queen,
reaching for her, opening his eyes in the murky brown
river.

His fingers closed on a scrap of her dress. Striking
his other hand out hard, he caught her arm and hauled
her to him. For a moment the cold deadweight of her
small china body seemed warm against his. Before he

could think too much about that, he was swimming toward the surface. His head broke through the waves, and he sucked in a grateful lungful of air.

His whole body was shaking with cold. His teeth chattered. His toes had gone numb. Behind him, Poppy and Alice were fighting, but it was hard to focus on their words.

Then the wake of the barge hit, the waves sending him under again, this time without him holding his breath. He came up choking.

The sailboat was at a strange angle, closer to shore. The waves had carried it to shallower water, where the keel caught in the mud. The *Pearl* had run aground.

The girls were wading through the shallow water.

They were shouting at each other, but Zach didn't pay attention. The water was too cold, and it took too much energy for him to do anything but put his head down and swim.

He kicked and kicked and kicked.

Clutching the Queen to his chest, leaving only a single free arm with which to paddle, reaching the shore seemed to take forever. And when he finally got there, the bank of the Ohio River was muddy, sucking at his feet, making wading ashore even harder than swimming had been.

Poppy was sitting on a fallen tree trunk, looking bedraggled and miserable. Her lips were blue with cold. Alice had sloughed off her coat somewhere and had her arms around herself like she was trying to physically restrain herself from shivering.

"The backpacks are gone," Alice said. "They must have fallen out when the boat rolled the first time."

Zach sank down on the sandy, muddy bank and looked at the doll in his arms. The Queen's dress was torn, and it seemed ready to disintegrate further as it dried. One of her arms had been pulled free from the socket and was hanging limply from a dirty string. He stared down at her and wondered why he'd been willing to jump back into a freezing river to get her.

He hadn't even thought about it. He didn't even remember deciding. He'd just known that if he didn't, he would lose something he wasn't ready to give up.

As the Queen's dull black eyes rolled up at him, he remembered what Poppy had said about breathing in the dead. Maybe when he'd opened up her bag of ashes, he'd inhaled some by accident. And if that was true, then maybe she could possess him anytime she wanted, just like the dead people who possessed you when you passed by graveyards. He wanted to drop her on the riverbank, but his hands wouldn't obey him.

"What time is it?" Alice asked. "My phone's dead."

He looked at his watch. The center of the crystal face had fogged up, but even if it had stopped, it couldn't be too far off. "Three twenty."

"We've got to get moving," Alice said, clearly panicked. "Get up. We've got to go."

Zach's feet felt like they were filled with lead. "Alice . . ." *We're not going to make it,* he wanted to tell her. *There's no way. We don't even know where we're going.* But he could see in her face that she already knew all those things. That she'd figured them out on the boat before she'd hurled the Queen into the waves.

"How could you—?" Poppy said to her, but then bit off the end of the sentence as Alice stalked off. Poppy pulled the doll from Zach's hands silently. He let her take it.

Alice walked with determination, and although Zach wasn't sure she knew where she was going, he and Poppy followed her.

They stumbled through the woods and then along the side of an empty stretch of road, past a raggedy wire fence that looked like it was keeping zombies back after an apocalypse rather than cows. As they tripped over rocks and stumps, wet hair sticking to their faces and necks, soaked socks squelching in their shoes, the silence stretched between them, making him even more panicked. Zach kept looking at his watch, which wasn't running entirely right anymore but still seemed to be ticking along faster than he wanted.

They were all shivering. Alice kept asking what time it was in a smaller and smaller voice. At three thirty, she kept marching with grim determination. At three thirty-four, she sped up to a near run. At three thirty-seven, she started to cry, quietly and to herself. He reached out a hand toward her, but she gave him such a terrible look that he pulled back and let her alone. At three forty-three, she set her jaw and kept going.

At three fifty-four, when the bus was well and truly gone, she whirled on Poppy.

"You promised this wouldn't happen!" she shouted. "You promised, and then you broke your promises over and over again, and now my whole life is going to be ruined because of you!"

"You never cared about the quest!" Poppy shouted back. "You threw Eleanor into the water. You threw her away like she was garbage."

"I thought maybe if she was gone, you'd go back to normal," Alice said. "I know you're just making all this up. Stop acting like it's so important, like you actually believe in it. Maybe you have Zach fooled, but you don't fool me."

"Is that what you're mad about? About Zach?"

"I don't—"

Poppy whirled on Zach. "She loooooves you. That's her big secret. She wants you to be her boyfriend and go to the movies with her and make kissy faces. That's the only reason she even came with us."

Zach took a step back, glancing over at Alice, expecting her to deny it.

Her trembling hands went to cover her face. She and Poppy were both shivering as hard as he was. But she didn't deny anything and he didn't have room in his brain to know how to process that. He felt a little embarrassed and a lot shocked. And it didn't matter anyway. They were all cold and miserable, and he had to do something before the fight they'd been having all along bubbled over into something so bad that it couldn't be taken back.

"Alice—" he started, not quite sure what he was going to say, but hoping he'd figure it out as he spoke.

She shook her head, keeping her eyes on Poppy. "Of course you would say that. You're horrible. Now I know why Zach is sick of you. He answered those Questions you gave him, you know. He obviously cares about the game, even if he's lying about it. He still wants to play. He just doesn't want to play with *you* anymore. And you know what? I don't either. He hates you, and I hate you too."

Then, as Poppy stared at her, stunned, her skin flushed in that blotchy way it got, Alice turned and ran from both of them. She pushed her way into the tangled brush of the woods.

"I don't hate you," Zach told Poppy. He hesitated a moment and then raced after Alice.

He knew he'd been the bad friend, the liar, the one that had started everybody fighting. He'd been hurt and mad and afraid of letting anyone see how he felt. But he'd thought they would go on being Poppy and Alice, playing the same game, being best friends, sleeping over at each other's houses.

He'd taken it for granted that he'd be able to go back to being friends later, if he wanted, and everything would be the way he'd left it. He'd counted on that.

But maybe he'd messed up everything.

It didn't take long to find Alice. She was sitting with her back against a tree, head tipped forward so that her wet braids hung in her face. He thought that maybe she'd been crying again, but he wasn't sure. The skin around her eyes was red and swollen.

"You didn't have to go looking for me," she said.

He went over and sat beside her. "Why did you say all that stuff?"

She shook her head, not looking up. "I don't know."

"You were really good on the boat. At sailing." Which sounded lame now that he heard the words out loud, although it had made sense in his head.

She shrugged. Zach had no idea how to make things better. He wanted to ask her if it was true that she liked him, but he didn't want to make her more upset—and since she'd gotten pretty upset already, it probably was true. But he wasn't sure why she'd been willing to follow Poppy onto the boat just to keep Zach from finding out. It wasn't an insult or anything. It was kind of a compliment.

Zach hadn't really thought about asking a girl out in any kind of real way, but if he was going to ask a girl out to get pizza or play video games, he'd want her to be like Alice.

The silence stretched until, unexpectedly, she broke it. "It *was* fun." She smiled lopsidedly. "Sailing. Even if we capsized. And I can't believe you *stole* that boat."

"We'll call the marina," he said, only a little defensively. "So it'll only be stolen for a little while."

She didn't reply, and he didn't want another moment of awkwardness. He gathered his courage. "I'm sorry—about everything. We should have gone back before. You were right. I'll tell your grandmother it was all our fault."

"It doesn't matter. That's not even what I'm really mad about." Alice leaned her head against the tree. "I mean, I am, but there's more."

He waited, unsure of what she was going to say next.

"Do you think there's a ghost that talks to Poppy?" Alice asked. "I'm not asking if you believe in ghosts. I'm asking if you believe in *this* ghost."

Zach nodded. "There was all that stuff with the donut guy and the crazy bus guy seeming to see her, and there was the camp getting messed up, and—and I had a dream about Eleanor last night in the woods. Just like Poppy. It wasn't the *same* dream, but it was *kind of* the same."

"You did?" Alice didn't look happy to hear it.

"I should have said something before," he told her.

"It's just—" Alice looked down at her hands. She clenched them. "I don't want to believe in Eleanor. I don't want there to be a ghost that's talking to Poppy—and now, to you."

"You can't really be jealous—"

She cut him off, talking very fast. "You don't understand. There can't be a ghost, a real ghost. Because if there is, then some random dead girl wants to haunt Poppy, but my own dead parents can't be bothered to come back and haunt me."

Everything seemed to pause, as though the universe had taken a moment to draw its breath.

Alice wiped her eyes with the back of one hand. They were wet and glittering with all the tears she was holding back. "What if we bury the Queen and Eleanor is really gone? What if we actually put her to rest? What if it's real? Does that mean that my parents didn't even care enough to say good-bye? I didn't even get a single stupid dream. Not *one*."

He remembered Alice's parents only vaguely. He recalled sitting on a linoleum floor, playing Matchbox cars with Alice in a sunny yellow kitchen while her mother made them toast with jam, her father wearing crazy ties to his job at the courthouse—and, of course, Zach remembered that they'd died. But he didn't think of them as dead, the way ghosts were dead. And he'd never thought about how it would be to go on a quest to dig a grave when your parents were already in one.

He felt like a jerk for not even considering it. Now

that he had, he wasn't sure there was anything he could say to Alice that wouldn't make him a bigger jerk. He was helpless.

"Maybe after we die, we don't get choices like that." He crouched down next to her. "And it probably sucks to be a ghost."

Alice snorted, the corner of her mouth lifting. "Maybe," she said.

Snapping twigs made them both look up. Zach stood. Poppy was walking toward them, wearing an uncomfortable expression, half relief and half dismay.

"I think I found the way to town," she said.

◌❧ CHAPTER THIRTEEN ❧◌

ALTHOUGH THE MAIN STREET OF EAST LIVERPOOL was full of big store windows and shops, many were no longer open at all. There was a place called Pants Unlimited that was covered in flyers advertising FINAL SALE! on everything, since they were going out of business, but by the aged look of the flyers, they might have been going out of business for years. The store owner stood in the doorway, smoking a cigarette. Zach and Poppy and Alice walked past him, still trailing water, their shoes making squelching sounds. Poppy hugged the Queen to her chest, the doll's face turned so that he couldn't see if her cheeks had grown even rosier. Next they passed a gaming store with a few bikes leaned against the pavement and a couple more chained to a

nearby STOP sign. And finally they came to a diner, the only restaurant they'd seen that was open.

They stopped to gaze at the menu on the door.

"I have four dollars and twenty-five cents—aside from the bus fare home," Zach said. "How much do you guys have?"

"That I can spend?" said Poppy. "Zero."

"Eight seventy-five," said Alice, pushing up her dress to rifle through the pockets of the jeans she had on underneath.

"So, not much before we start dipping into our bus fare home," Poppy said. "But something."

Alice looked grim at the mention of the bus, but didn't say anything, which was good, but also made Zach nervous. All the way from the woods, the three of them had only said things having to do with figuring out where they were going. He couldn't decide if the girls didn't want to fight anymore or if they were gearing up for an even bigger fight that was about to come.

Somehow he'd become at the center of their conflict, and he could tell it was just a matter of time before they figured out that they didn't have to be mad at each other—he was the one they should both be mad at. He was the one who had messed up the game, the one who had hidden the Questions, the one who Alice—

The one who Alice liked, which was weird too. It wasn't like he hadn't thought about girls or even like he'd never thought about Alice *like that*. He had. But actually asking her out? The idea was paralyzing.

"Okay," Zach said, pushing open the door to the diner. "Let's go in."

The diner was warm, with a round display of desserts near the register that turned, showing huge cakes and pies piled with icing and oozing filling. There were little glass dishes of Jell-O and others of rice pudding studded with raisins, each one covered in plastic wrap.

A woman standing behind the register, her white hair in short beauty-parlor curls, looked them up and down skeptically, as though she was trying to decide if they were trouble. "You can't track mud all over the place," she said finally.

Zach could smell something frying in the back, and his stomach lurched with hunger.

"Sorry," said Alice, taking a step forward, putting on her best acting face. "We were out racing our sailboat and got really into it. A little too much, I guess. We just wanted to get something warm to eat before we go back. The water was really cold."

The woman behind the register smiled, like the idea of healthy outdoor activity had made their mud-stained appearance wholesome. Or maybe she figured that kids with sailboats had money, however bad they looked. "Well, okay, but you go dry off in the back first. Table for four?"

"Three," Alice said, and the woman blinked in confusion.

Zach narrowed his eyes at the doll, hanging limply in Poppy's arms.

"Come on." Poppy took Alice's arm and hauled her toward the bathrooms. As she walked she looked back at the white-haired woman at the register. "Table for four is fine."

Zach went into the men's bathroom. There was a row of three urinals and a single stall, all in baby-blue tile, with paintings of the Ohio River in the olden days hanging high on the walls. He walked over to the sinks, took off his shoes, and rinsed them off. Then he took off his jeans, wiped dirt and bits of grass from the cuffs, and tried to dry them the best he could with a combination of paper towels and a hand dryer.

Finally he wrung out his shirt over one of the sinks, hand-combed his wet hair, and put his jeans back on. They stuck to his legs, damp and chill. He looked back into the mirror, seeing a slightly sunburnt boy looking back at him, older than he remembered himself, with a familiar mess of brown-black hair and black eyes that seemed to say: *I hope you know what you're doing.*

When he left the bathroom, Alice and Poppy were already sitting in a banquette. They waved in his direction, and he slid in just as their waitress arrived.

She was only a little older than they were, with pink lipstick, blunt-cut black hair, and a nose ring. Handing over the menus, she paused to stare at the Queen, lolling beside Poppy.

"Your doll?" the waitress said, pointing. Dirt from the riverbed was in the grooves of her nose and mouth and was turning her blond ringlets into thick clumps. "Superscary."

"Oh, yeah," said Alice, with a dark look in Poppy's direction. "The scariest."

The waitress smiled, handed them the menus, and walked off. Zach was just glad that it seemed like she was seeing a *doll*, instead of whatever Tinshoe Jones, the donut guy, and the lady at the register had seen. He pushed the thought out of his mind and studied the menu. They had twelve seventy-five that they could spend and still get home—and that was budgeting on loaning Poppy a quarter for her bus fare.

There were biscuits and eggs in white sausage gravy with hash browns, maybe big enough for them to split two plates three ways, for five dollars. But there was also a turkey bacon club sandwich that came with fries and slaw for a little more than seven dollars, and if they got water with that instead of sodas, and figured on a tip of a dollar, they would still have money left over. And there was the three eggs with hash browns and toast for three ninety-five—just enough that they couldn't afford it all around.

There was a bowl of chili for two ninety-five that seemed promising. You could get a side of fries for another two fifty. Maybe if they got three orders of chili and one side of fries?

Thinking about what they could afford to eat was making his mouth water. If they didn't figure out something soon, he was going to order it all and have no way home.

"Be right back," Alice said, and headed off toward the counter, leaving him alone at the table with Poppy.

"Maybe you should go after her," Zach said. "Talk."

"Maybe *you* should go after her," Poppy told him, pushing loose strands of wet hair behind her ears.

Zach sighed. "Don't be like that."

"Don't be like what?" She stared at him unblinkingly. "Are you going to tell me why you answered all those Questions and then lied about it? Why you wouldn't play even one more time?"

"I *couldn't*," Zach said.

"That doesn't make any sense." She folded her arms and balanced her chin on them, watching him.

"I know," he said miserably. "I thought it would be easier—"

He broke off as Alice came back to the table, holding a bottle of ketchup and another bottle of hot sauce. She opened her menu, scanning the prices.

"There are free refills on the sodas," she said. "We could get one and share it."

"And be out a dollar seventy-five," Zach said.

"I asked about the bus, too," Alice said, not looking at any of them. "Next one comes tomorrow, same time as today. I got directions to the stop. It's a couple miles from here."

Zach wondered if it was closer to where they'd fallen into the river, whether they'd gone the wrong way, whether they could have made it after all, but he didn't ask. Poppy was silent, worrying her lower lip with her teeth. The Queen's dark eyes shone in her mud-streaked face, and Zach couldn't help thinking that everything was going exactly the way she wanted it to, even if he had no proof of that.

They were still studying the menu when the waitress came back around to take their drink order (tap water) and placed a basket of bread and margarine on the table. They fell on it, ripping apart the rolls, spreading them with margarine, and stuffing them into their mouths.

Zach felt better, having eaten something since the donut. Poppy and Alice must have felt better too, because they were able to agree on the chili and fries, which they devoured down to the last little burnt, ketchup-and-hot-sauce-covered crisp of fry.

"I'm so tired," Alice said, putting her head down on the table. "All the walking and the swimming and the being cold and miserable. I could go to sleep right here. Seriously, under this table. It would be more comfortable than sleeping on the ground was."

"We're almost done," Poppy said softly. "We've almost made it."

"I know," Alice said, groaning. "I'm stuck here, so I'm in for finishing the quest. But are we seriously going to a cemetery at night and digging a grave?"

Zach looked out the window at the street. The sun was still in the sky, but it wouldn't be for long. Alice was right. By the time they figured out where they were going and actually got there, it would probably be pretty late.

"If we are going to go tonight, we need to get supplies," said Zach. "Something to dig with and a flashlight. All that stuff was in our backpacks, and now it's at the bottom of the Ohio River."

Alice inhaled sharply, and Zach followed her gaze. She was staring at the doll. Its head was turned, like it was looking out the window. Poppy was looking in the same direction, mirroring the doll's pose perfectly.

"*Poppy,*" he said. "Stop messing around."

"What?" she turned back to look at them, like she was oblivious. He hadn't seen her turn the Queen's head toward the window, but she must have. The doll didn't move on its own—had never left the case, needed them to bring it to the grave. It *didn't move.*

He really hoped it didn't move.

Except for that time in the woods.

"You know where we're going, right? You know which cemetery we're going to, right?" He thought back to the moment before they got on the bus back home and how he'd asked her almost the same thing. *The grave is under a willow tree. Eleanor will tell us the rest.*

Alice looked about to say something scathing.

Poppy nodded, not looking at either of them. "Yeah."

"You do, *right*?" Alice asked.

"Of course," Poppy said, meeting their eyes, looking from Zach to Alice. "I just need a map."

Zach would have liked her to seem more confident, but then he would have liked her to stop being so crazy about the Queen and also maybe to stop acting like she might be occasionally possessed. Zach would have liked a lot of things.

They paid the check with everything but the bus fare home, dumping the grimy pennies from the bottom of their pockets on the other coins and bills. The waitress smiled at them on the way out, and Zach smiled back, even though he knew they were completely broke.

"Hey," Alice said, reaching down past circulars and coupon flyers near the door to pick up a crude tourist map. It didn't have any graveyards on it, but it did have the pottery museum, a few antique pottery stores, and the Carnegie Library. "Is this any good?"

"The library," Zach said. "They'll have really detailed maps. We could use this to get there."

According to the tourist map, the library wasn't far. Now that she was a bit more dry and had eaten something, Alice seemed almost cheerful. He guessed that at this point there was no way she wasn't getting in trouble, so maybe she'd just stopped worrying about it. She took the lead, Poppy trailing behind Zach, holding the Queen as though the doll had become very heavy. They walked down a few blocks until the library came into view, its stately front looking out onto the water. It was domed on top, with red stone making up the body and carved white stone trimming on the windows.

It looked out of place, too grand for what surrounded it. It was also closed. It had been closed since one in the afternoon and wasn't due to open again until Monday morning.

"Who closes a library on the weekend?" Poppy said, kicking one of the steps softly with the toe of her shoe.

Zach shrugged, then turned to see what Alice thought. She was crouched near a basement window, pushing on the glass.

"What are you doing?" he whispered.

The window slid up a little ways, and Alice wedged her boot into the open space, scrambling to push it higher. It seemed stuck; probably the wood had swollen from changes in temperature and being unopened for years. "What does it look like?" she said.

"Breaking into a government-owned building that we could get *arrested* for being inside of."

"Yup," she said as the window slid up abruptly with a squeal. "That's exactly what I'm doing."

"Well," Poppy said. "Okay then."

Alice shimmied inside, hesitating once she was perched on the inner sill. The room was too shadowed for them to see what she was about to drop down onto.

"Alice," Zach said warningly.

She jumped. There was a crash and a sound like something metal hitting the floor.

"Alice!" Poppy yelped.

"Shhhhh," Alice called back from the darkness, smugness filling her voice. "See, I'm not so bad at quests after all."

"That was amazing," Zach said. "Exactly what Lady Jaye would do."

"Well, come on then, William." Alice's voice, from the dark, was eerily changed. It was like he was talking to Alice and the character she played at the same time. For a moment he wasn't sure who that made him. And in that moment he wasn't sure who he wanted to be either, but he was grinning like an idiot.

He glanced back at Poppy. She looked crushed, like she was on the outside of a glass looking in at something she wanted desperately. They were playing, and he could tell she knew that if she tried to play too, he'd stop. For a moment he felt bad, but he was too happy to feel that way for long. It was fun to act like William with Alice, and it was fun to sneak into a building in the middle of the day, when even scary things weren't that frightening.

"What did you land on?" he called to Alice, moving to slide his legs through.

"Desk," she said. "Wait a second."

He heard rustling and something else tip over, crashing and hitting the floor. Then the lights flickered to life, revealing a room filled with metal desks and filing cabinets, their surfaces covered in mounds of paper. Some kind of administrative storage area.

Zach kicked off the wall, jumping wide of the desk that Alice had probably hit; paper was scattered around it, and one of its desk lamps was lying just above the floor, dangling from a cord. He landed near a tall filing cabinet, nearly stumbling into it as he tried not to lose his balance.

"Wow, what is all this stuff?" he asked, walking through the space. Books were piled up next to lamps and old black-and-white photographs of the town in tidy black frames with engraved plates. A bookshelf had been shoved against the back wall, and one of the shelves was filled with old pottery.

It was exhilarating to be somewhere they weren't supposed to be. Like being on the boat. A real adventure, like William and Lady Jaye would have had.

"Hey! Come take Eleanor," Poppy called, holding out the doll as she shimmied down through the window.

He did, putting the Queen on top of one of the cabinets. Lying on her side, the doll's eyes watched Zach accusingly as he helped Poppy down. As he did, a gust of cold wind blew through the room, scattering papers.

"We're not going to be able to close that without a ladder," Alice said, pointing at the window. "It's too high up."

"We won't be here long," said Poppy, picking up the Queen and walking toward the door.

Zach bumped his arm against Alice's as they followed her. "I guess you're not going to loot the place, huh, Jaye?"

"Let's wait and see what we find upstairs," she told him, grinning, as they stepped into the darkened hall.

The basement of the library was warm and smelled like wood polish and old paper. Zach inhaled deeply. He felt like he could relax for the first time since they'd gotten on the bus. They weren't cold and exposed like they'd been outside, and they weren't in front of people who could get them in trouble, the way they had been in the donut shop and at the diner, or hanging on for their lives, like they'd been on the boat.

Plus there was so much to see. They explored the conference room, the bathrooms, and two more storage rooms on the basement level. There was an exhibit of china vases behind glass, and the whole cabinet shook gently as they ran past.

Then they jogged up the steps and saw the vaulted ceilings, iron railings, and marble of the main floor. According to a legend on the wall, Carnegie was a famous philanthropist who'd been born super poor in a small Scottish town, made money in steel and used it to build libraries on the East Coast, among other good-deed-type things. In the picture, he looked like an angry old man with a short beard.

He didn't look like the kind of guy who liked stories, but Zach thought he must have had to, to have built so many libraries.

"Hey," Poppy said, calling to him from the second floor, where there was a rotunda that looked down on the reference desk on the first floor. "Come check this out!"

He grinned and ran for the stairs, quest forgotten.

There was something about being alone in an empty building. There was something about racing up the stairs and hanging over the balcony, your shout bouncing off the walls. Zach and Poppy and Alice dashed through the upstairs gallery, through the big rooms. And without really ever saying so, they started playing. Not their old game, which was still contentious, although Alice and Zach slipping into those characters on the way in made it easier to slip into new ones. First Poppy and Zach pretended to be monsters hiding in their library lair when Alice as monster-hunter came in. She chased them around for a while, trying to slay them, before they ganged up and chased her back, threatening to turn her into a monster too. They slid across the floor in their stocking feet, hiding behind stacks and riding on the book carts, shrieking as they went.

When they got tired of that, they went behind the back of the reference desk and rifled through the drawers, finding—in addition to pens, pencils, a flash drive, and a bunch of rubber bands—a pair of silver hoop earrings, a mystery novel with the cover ripped off, and an eraser in the shape of a delete key. At the desk Zach was even able to call the marina and leave the promised message about the boat while Poppy looked on.

Alice found a break room with a small kitchenette. There was a coffeepot, tea bags and sugar packets, and a refrigerator that contained five slightly wrinkly apples, a low-fat yogurt, a dry-looking hunk of cheddar, and a nearly full package of Oreos. Four folding chairs surrounded a table covered in review copies of books that hadn't been released yet.

"Look at this!" Poppy held up a book they'd all been waiting for—one that wasn't due out for months.

"And no one's going to be in until Monday," Zach said, sitting in one of the chairs and stretching out, dumping his damp jacket onto the table. "We can sleep here tonight. We are going to be warm and dry, and it's going to be amazing."

Alice snickered. He smiled up at the ceiling stupidly.

"We still have to go to the graveyard, remember?" Poppy stood, all the giddy joy draining out of her. "We can't get comfortable."

And just like that, all the fun of running around the library was over. Alice's mouth pressed into a thin, resentful line as Poppy stalked off toward the main room. Their feud was back on.

He sighed. It was true that he didn't want to go out into the cold either. And now that the end of the quest was so close, some part of him didn't want it to be over. He didn't want to go out into the graveyard and find out there wasn't any magic after all. It seemed easier to goof around in the stacks and worry about burying the Queen in the morning.

Alice looked after Poppy, scowling.

Zach stood up, pacing the small room. "You guys have to make up. You're friends. You're supposed to be friends. You can't just not talk, or talk in the weird not-talking way you've both been."

Alice shook her head. "You don't understand. It's just—it's easy for Poppy. She wants this one thing, and I better want it too. Either I'm with her or against her, you know? And she's like that about everything."

"I don't think it's easy for her," Zach said.

Alice sighed. "If she wants to be friends, then she can say so. I get that the quest is important, but it seems like maybe it's the *only* important thing."

Zach sighed again and opened the door to the main room of the library.

He found Poppy at a long table, where she'd spread out several maps, an atlas, and a guidebook. She was standing on a chair, looking down on all of it. The Queen was resting at one end, lying on her side, limp arms outstretched.

"Did you find it?" Zach asked.

She turned with a start. She must not have heard him come in.

"Here," she said, stepping onto the table and walking over to one of the maps, where she crouched down and pointed. "Spring Grove Cemetery."

"You're sure?" asked Alice, and it was Zach's turn to be surprised. He hadn't expected that she would follow him.

"I didn't have an aerial view in my dreams, but it

looks right," Poppy said. "We should go tonight. There might be streetlights down there, and the moon is pretty full. Even without a flashlight, I think we can find her grave. And then it's over. I promise."

Alice rolled her eyes.

"I'll copy the map," Poppy said.

"Okay," said Zach. "Get me when you're ready." He picked up a book of local history that Poppy must have pulled from the stacks, and walked off toward a couple of couches he'd spotted near the picture-book section.

Flopping down, he flipped through the book, skimming over the section on local folklore. There wasn't any mention of an Eleanor Kerchner or a haunted doll, but there was a story about a Dutch girl who haunted a canal lock and a creepy little boy who hung himself. And there was a lady who got stood up on her wedding day and was found, weeks later, dead in her wedding gown. Legend had it that her bleached white skeleton ran around playing in traffic and grabbing people. When Zach got bored, he slipped pieces of paper, on which he'd written cryptic words, between the pages.

A little while later he heard the quiet murmur of voices and hoped that meant that Poppy and Alice were making up. He thought that maybe he would just close his eyes for a second.

After all, they were going to be digging up a grave, and they were going to have to do it with scissors or sticks or whatever other tools they could find. It was going to be hard work. But it was going to get done; Zach was sure about that. So he needed to rest a little. He leaned back on the couch, turning his cheek against the crook of his arm.

This time he dreamed that he was lying on a lawn, looking up at a big house. He couldn't get his legs to move. There was something wrong with his vision. It was darkening at the edges, but he could see enough to notice that there were shattered remains of porcelain dolls all around him.

And then he heard a voice, which he knew to be Eleanor's father. "She looks just like one of them. She looks just like a broken doll."

When he woke up, a woman he didn't know was standing over him. She looked like she was about to scream, but he beat her to it.

❧ CHAPTER FOURTEEN ❧

THE WOMAN BROUGHT HER THIN ARMS UP DEFEN-
sively, as though his shouting was some kind of attack.
He scrabbled up onto the couch and then over it, landing on the other side. She blinked owlishly behind her
bright-green glasses. She was about his mother's age,
with short, curly, bright-pink hair.

Above her, light streamed in from the windows.
It was Sunday morning. He'd slept through the whole
night.

Looking around, he spotted Poppy and Alice lying
on the other couch, heads pillowed on opposite sides.
They were both opening their eyes. Poppy pushed herself up.

"Who are you?" Zach asked the woman.

"I work here," she said. "I'm a librarian. I came in on the weekend, like I always do—I have to do my orders for new books, and it's easier when there aren't any patrons. Now, do you want to tell me what you three are doing here? And are you alone? I thought I heard something downstairs."

"Um," Zach said, still dazed from sleep. Answers deserted him.

"It's just us," said Alice, rubbing her face. "We left the window open. You probably heard the wind."

The librarian peered at the three of them more

closely. "You're lucky I didn't immediately call the police. How old are you?"

His brain was finally catching up to what was going on, and he realized just how much trouble they were in. "Twelve," he said.

She turned to Alice and Poppy. "Where exactly do your parents think you are?"

Alice shrugged.

"Well, we're going to go into the office and we're going to call them right now, okay? And you better not have vandalized this place, or I'm going to change my mind and call the cops after all."

"We didn't mess up anything," Poppy said. "Look around and see if we're telling the truth, and then if we are, you can let us go. We won't be any more trouble."

"It's either we call your parents," the pink-haired librarian said, "or we call the police."

Adrenaline spiked through Zach. He considered running. If they all sprinted for the doors, he was pretty certain they'd make it. Alice's shoes were off, which was a problem, but maybe she could grab them. And then there was the doll. Poppy didn't seem to be holding her, which was unusual. He thought about the last time he'd woken up and found the Queen not where she'd been the night before, but when he glanced around the library, nothing else seemed amiss. The couches hadn't been ripped; there was no scattered stuffing and no tossed packages of food from the break room.

By that point, though, he'd lost his chance. The librarian was waving them up off the couches, and he couldn't catch either girl's eye, so if he ran, he wasn't sure they'd follow.

"Come on in the back and I'll make you a cup of tea," the pink-haired librarian said. "You all look like you could use it."

They must have seemed pretty scruffy as they shuffled to the break room in the same clothes they'd been wearing for a day and two nights. The cat ears on Alice's hoodie were bent at odd angles, and there was ink smeared across Poppy's cheek, like maybe one of the pens she'd been using had started to bleed. Zach wondered if the librarian thought they were homeless kids. He wondered if telling her they were would make her let them go.

Halfway across the library floor, Poppy stopped. "Wait, where's the Queen?" Her voice was high-pitched, panicked.

"You don't know?" Zach asked. He looked around again, as though somehow the doll was going to materialize out of the ether.

The librarian raised her eyebrows, as though waiting for an explanation.

"A doll," Zach said. "She's really old. Poppy must have lost her."

"Well, where did you have her last?" Alice asked Poppy.

"I brought her with me when I went to the couch," she said. "I know I did. She was *right there* next to me when I went to sleep."

"Before that, she was on the map table," Zach put in. "Maybe you forgot—"

"I saw the doll," Alice interrupted, "when we went to sleep. *Someone* must have gotten up and moved her."

Poppy started to go look when the librarian caught her arm.

"All of you," she said with an impressive firmness. "You will go into the break room, and then we'll deal with the missing doll and your parents and everything else. The library is closed. If the doll is here, we'll find it. Meanwhile, it's not going anywhere. Now, let's go."

Zach really *hoped* the doll wasn't going anywhere.

They sat down on folding chairs around the breakroom table as the librarian put on the electric kettle. She looked through the cabinets until she found a package of Fig Newtons, which she ripped open and put in front of them.

"I'm Katherine Rausse," she said. "You may call me Miss Katherine. Not Kathy, *Katherine*."

"I'm Poppy," Poppy said. "Poppy Bell. And this is Alice Magnaye and Zachary Barlow."

"Very melodic names," said the librarian, pulling mugs out of a cupboard. The water had heated quickly, so she was able to take out tea bags, drop one in each mug, and fill them with boiling water. Steam rose from each, along with the comforting smell of bruised leaves. "We don't have milk, but I'll put the sugar on the table. Now, I am going to call my director and inform her of what's going on. I am going to lock this door, but I will be right back, so if you need to use the bathroom or anything, I promise that I will take you as soon as I return."

She went out, leaving them alone, the click of the latch signaling that she wasn't kidding about locking them inside.

Zach had no idea how they were going to get out of the break room. No idea how they were going to find the Queen. No idea how they were going to do anything but go home in disgrace, their quest forever undone. The idea of stopping now, though, when they were so close, grated on Zach. It drove him nuts that if they'd just gone to the graveyard last night—if he'd just been less lazy—the quest might be over and done.

Poppy peered at her mug. Then, abruptly, she wiped her eyes with the back of one hand. "I'm sorry," she said.

Alice sighed. "It's not your fault. I'm the one who broke in."

"And I'm the one who fell asleep," Zach said. "You're the one who kept reminding us, Poppy. It's not your fault—"

Poppy cut him off. "That's not what I mean. I thought that we could do this thing, and when it was over we'd have something that no one else had—an experience that would keep us together. I can see you changing." She turned to Zach. "You're going to be one of those guys who hangs out with their teammates and dates cheerleaders and doesn't remember what it was like to make up stuff. And you—" She whirled on Alice. "You're going to be too busy thinking about boys and trying out for school plays and whatever to remember. It's like you're both forgetting everything. You're forgetting who you are. I thought this would remind you. And I'm sorry because it was stupid. I was stupid."

"That's not fair," Alice said.

"Yeah, I didn't *forget*," said Zach. Poppy sounded just like his dad, except in reverse. He didn't want to forget, and he wanted everyone to stop talking like it was inevitable, like it would happen whether he wanted it to or not.

Alice rolled her eyes. "We're not zombies just because we like stuff you don't."

"No, you're right," Poppy said, her voice speeding up and getting louder, like she was afraid she was going to be cut off before she got it all out. "It's *not fair*. We had a story, and our story was important. And I hate that both of you can just walk away and take part of my story with you and not even care. I hate that you can do what you're supposed to do and I can't. I hate that you're going to leave me behind. I hate that everyone calls it growing up, but it seems like *dying*. It feels like each of you is being possessed and I'm next."

Zach and Alice were quiet for a long moment.

Before they could speak, the door opened and Miss Katherine came in. Her glasses were hanging around her neck from a chain, and she looked a little nervous. "Well," she said, "the director wants me to tell you that if there's something wrong at home, we can call social services instead of your parents."

There was a long silence.

"I am going to assume that means we're going with the original plan." She nodded to herself, her pink curls bouncing as she did. "Now, who wants to call home first?"

Alice stood up, pushing her chair back. "I'll go. My grandmother's probably worried."

"You sure?" Poppy said. "I can call first if you want."

Alice gave her a withering look. "No, that's okay. Don't do me any favors."

When they were gone, Zach drank his tea and ate five Fig Newtons, although they tasted like nothing in his mouth. He chewed and swallowed automatically.

"Are you mad at me?" Poppy asked.

"No," Zach said. Then, after considering it a little more, "Maybe."

"How much trouble do you think she's going to get in?" Poppy asked him.

"Lots," he said, putting his head down on his arms.

She slumped at the table and rested her head in a gesture that mirrored his. He thought about the way they'd all been friends for so long that they even shared mannerisms. He thought about how they'd met, years ago.

He thought about what Poppy had said about growing up and losing themselves.

And how bad it would be if Alice got in so much trouble that they could never see her again.

And how awful it would be if Alice and Poppy never made up.

He thought about what his mother and father were going to say when he called, and what he could possibly say back.

He thought about the stories, all the stories. The ones they'd made up and the ones they never had.

He was still thinking about those things when the door opened and Alice came back in, wearing shoes. She looked grim.

"Okay, Poppy," Miss Katherine said. "Your turn."

Poppy stood up and went out with only a single glance back.

"How was it?" Zach asked Alice after a long moment. She had been fiddling with the electric kettle switch, turning it on and then off again, seeming lost in thought.

"Oh," she said. "Weird. My aunt Linda was there. Grandma had called her. She'd wanted to go out looking for me yesterday after I didn't come back, but she knew she couldn't see very well at night. She was mad, but—I don't know, she sounded different. Like she realized she was old for the first time."

"You think you're going to be grounded forever?" Zach asked.

"Oh, yeah," Alice said. "Forever and a day. Even if she lets Aunt Linda help out more."

He didn't want to never see Alice again. Before he chickened out, he blurted out the words. "So if I asked you to go to the movies with me or something—"

She leaned against the counter, glancing over at him, a smile lifting one corner of her mouth. "Are you asking me out?"

"Yeah," he said, wiping his hands against his jeans. His palms had started to sweat. "Yes. Will you—"

"Yes," she cut him off, saying the word very quickly, not looking at him. He wondered if she felt as awkward as he did. He was glad he asked and he was glad she said yes, but he was also glad she was grounded, so it wouldn't be happening soon.

The door opened, and they both jumped. Poppy came in and threw herself into one of the folding chairs. She looked, if anything, even more upset than Alice had.

"You okay?" Zach asked.

"I need a ride," Poppy mumbled, putting her head in her hands again.

"What?" Alice asked.

"I couldn't get my dad, and my mom's working until late. She asked if one of your folks could drive me."

Miss Katherine topped up her cup with more hot water. "Zachary, it's your turn."

He stood and walked toward the door. As he was going out he looked back at Poppy. Alice was standing behind her chair, hand on her shoulder. And in that moment he realized that he didn't want them to have to go back never having completed the quest. He wanted them to finish this thing the way Poppy had imagined: together.

He watched as the librarian locked the break-room door. Then he followed her through the library to an office on the third floor, where there was a small desk, piled with more review copies of books and papers, scattered with pens. A folding chair with a padded seat rested in front of it and a cloth chair on wheels behind it.

"Have a seat," she said, sitting down behind the desk. She picked up the phone and handed it over to him. "You dial the number, but I need to talk to your parents. I'll tell them where you are, and then I'll hand you the phone. I'll go outside to give you some privacy unless you want me to stay here, okay?"

He nodded.

He reminded himself that he wouldn't care if they were upset. He was still mad about what his dad had done and how little his mother had cared. If he kept that in the front of his thoughts, then nothing they could say would bother him. He just wouldn't care.

He wiped his hands against his jeans and hoped it was true. He dialed and handed the phone over.

The librarian took the receiver and started explaining how she'd found Zach sleeping on the couch in the Carnegie Public Library in East Liverpool—yes, East Liverpool, Ohio—and yes, he was fine, he had two friends with him, and they were fine too. She gave the address of the library and some abbreviated directions.

Then she held out the phone to him.

Zach took it and brought it slowly to his ear as Miss Katherine went out the door, closing it softly behind her. "Mom?" Zach said.

"It's me," said his father. "You all right?"

Zach's heart sped. "Yeah, like she said. I'm fine."

"I never meant to make you feel like you had to run away," Zach's dad said softly. As soon as his father had picked up, Zach had expected a lot of shouting and the phone getting slammed in its cradle. But his father didn't sound angry. Zach wasn't sure why, but more than anything else, his dad sounded scared.

"That's not what I was doing," he said. "I was on a quest. I was going to come back when I was finished."

Once Zach said the words, he knew they were true. He would have gone back. He'd just needed a little break.

There was a long pause on the other end of the line, as though his father was not quite sure how to respond. "So, this quest," he said finally, tentatively. "Are you done with it now?"

"Not yet," said Zach. "I thought I was, but—I don't think that I am."

"We're going to get in the car, and we're going to be there in two and a half hours. Do you think you'll be finished then?"

"I don't know."

"Your mother's been real worried. You want to talk to her?"

Zach wanted to tell her that everything was okay, that he was fine, but he didn't want to hear her voice and realize how much he'd upset her. "No," he said after a moment. "See you when you get here."

His father gave a heavy sigh. "You know I don't understand you."

"You don't have to." Zach just wanted the conversation over, before either of them said something awful.

"I *want* to," his father said.

Zach snorted.

There was a long silence on the other end of the line. "I'm not good at this kind of thing, but even though I don't always get things and your mother tells me I don't know how to talk, I wanted to tell you that I've been thinking about what I did with those toys ever since it happened. It was a mean thing to do. I grew up mean, and I don't want you to have to grow up mean too."

Zach was silent. He'd never heard his father talk that way before.

"When I saw you with those figures, I pictured you getting hassled at school. I thought you needed to be tougher. But I've been thinking that protecting somebody by hurting them before someone else gets the chance isn't the kind of protecting that anybody wants."

"Yeah," Zach said. It was all he could bring himself to say. He had no idea his father thought about anything like this. All the anger had drained out of him, leaving him feeling as fragile as one of those paper-thin china cups.

"So I'll see you soon," his father told him. "Good luck with the quest." He said the word as though it was a strange, unfamiliar shape in his mouth, but he said it.

"Bye, Dad," said Zach, and hung up the phone.

He sat there for a long moment, breathing hard. Something had shifted, something seismic, and he needed to be still long enough to have it settle inside of him. Then he stood up and went out the door.

ᏂᎤᏍ CHAPTER FIFTEEN ᏂᎤᏍ

MISS KATHERINE WAS SHELVING A FEW BOOKS NEARBY and put them back on the cart when he emerged from the office. Her pink hair was as bright as the synthetic mane of a plastic horse.

"Everything okay?" she asked him.

"They're coming," Zach said, trying to put the strangeness of his father's words behind him. "Did you see Poppy's doll?"

She shook her head. "I walked by the table where you left all those maps, but there was nothing else there. Do you want to take a look yourself?"

Zach nodded and followed her to the couches. He noticed her shoes for the first time, bright yellow with bows. She didn't look like any librarian he'd ever seen before. In fact, she didn't look like any adult he'd met before.

Zach looked under the sofa the girls had slept on and then under the one where he'd fallen asleep—after all, the last time he'd woken up, the doll was resting right next to his head. He knelt down with a shudder at the thought of her lying directly underneath where he'd slept, as though she might reach up her tiny porcelain hands and drag him down *through* the couch cushions. She wasn't there, though.

The Queen wasn't under the table, either. She wasn't in any of the chairs, nor anywhere obvious on the rug. She wasn't anywhere he could see.

He didn't *feel* her either, didn't sense the gaze of her dull eyes watching him from some corner of the room, the way he had when she was in the cabinet in Poppy's living room.

While he searched, Miss Katherine started gathering up the books and maps Poppy had left on the table the night before.

"What was it that you kids were trying to find?" the librarian asked, frowning at him. He could tell that Miss Katherine didn't know what to make of the story about the doll. He wasn't sure that she even believed there *was* a doll. If not, he wondered what she thought he was looking for.

He shrugged. "Nothing."

"It looks like someone was doing research on a cemetery near here," said Miss Katherine gently. "Spring Grove? I saw a few pieces of copy paper with directions drawn on them and scratched out. What's in Spring Grove Cemetery? You can tell me, Zach. I promise that I'll try to understand."

"Have you ever heard a story, a ghost story, about a girl who jumped off her roof?" He hesitated, pressing the front of his sneaker against one of the legs of the table. He wanted to trust her, but he knew he couldn't trust her *too* much—she'd never believe him if he told her everything. "Like under mysterious circumstances? Maybe one named Eleanor Kerchner."

Miss Katherine shook her head. "The only Kerchner I can think of was a fancy worker—a very well-known potter locally. We even have a display of his work downstairs, courtesy of the museum. There was a grisly story about him, but I don't know about any Eleanor Kerchner."

That felt a little too real, there being a potter with a grisly story.

"Downstairs?" Zach took a few steps across the library floor before Miss Katherine cleared her throat.

"I don't think so," Miss Katherine said. "I let you

look around, but enough's enough. Come on."

Zach remembered the wall of fragile-looking vases he'd seen in the basement. He'd run past them, not really looking at them, and now he was itching to know what he'd missed. He had to get down there. He had to. His heart started to pound with renewed hope. Maybe there was a secret there—a secret that might not help them to finish the quest but would prove that it was a real one. A real quest for a real ghost.

He concentrated on that as the librarian led him back to the break room and opened the door with the key sticking out of the lock. Inside, the girls were sitting at opposite ends of the table wearing near-identical expressions of worry.

"I am going to call the director back," Miss Katherine said, with a bright smile that might have been forced. "Let her know that everything's been resolved. Then we'll figure out some lunch for you kids. It's almost noon."

"Thank you," Alice said quietly.

"Thank you," Poppy and Zach echoed automatically.

The librarian went out, and Zach waited until he heard the turn of the key in the lock. Then he put both his hands palm down on the table, like he was going to give a speech.

"Okay," he said, looking from one friend to the other. "We need a plan. We need to break out of this room before the librarian comes back."

Alice stood up, looking a little confused, but hopeful. "How?"

"It doesn't matter," Poppy said, staying seated. "We don't have the Queen anymore. Even if we get out of here—and I have no idea how we could do that—we can't finish the quest without her."

"We'll find her," said Zach. "I looked around where we were sleeping, and she wasn't there, but that doesn't mean anything. We can find her. We can do this. Are you sure you didn't bring her with you anywhere else? Anywhere?"

Poppy shook her head. It seemed to Zach that giving them that speech about all the stuff she hated had drained away the part of her that had driven her this far. Or maybe it was losing the Queen. Either way, Poppy looked more defeated than he'd ever seen her. "No. When I sat down on the couch, she was with me. I was worried about rolling over on her, since she's so fragile, so I put her on the floor and hung my hand down to keep touching her. I would have known if someone moved her."

"Creepy," Alice said. "What is it with you and the

Queen? You're always holding her and touching her. Don't you find the whole she-was-made-from-human-bones thing even a little bit, like, scary?"

Poppy gave her a look.

"I don't mean it like that," said Alice. "Not like you're being weird. Are you sure she's not doing something to you? *Making you* act like what she wants?"

"Oh, so *now* you believe in the possibility of a ghost," Poppy sneered.

"We'll find the Queen," Zach insisted, interrupting before they started fighting again. "Just as soon as we figure a way out of this room. Which we will. In just a second an idea is going to come to me, and it's going to be a good one." He leaned against the wall, folding his arms and trying to concentrate. They could tell Miss Katherine they had to go to use the bathroom—all of them at the same time—and then sneak out the window. The only problem was that Miss Katherine probably wouldn't let them all use the bathroom at once. Well, that and the fact that the windows in the basement were really far up the wall; they'd had to drop down during the climb in. And just one more problem—he wasn't sure there *was* a window in the girls' bathroom.

Alice stared up at the ceiling. Then she stepped

onto one of the folding chairs, and from there onto the table.

"What are you doing?" Poppy asked.

Alice went up on her toes and shoved at one of the ceiling tiles. It moved over, showing the metal grid that suspended it. Beyond was only darkness, like the gap left by a missing tooth. "I have an idea," she said. "Look at how low the ceiling is in here. And look at the door—it's different from the others; the knob is really shiny."

"So?" Zach said, walking over and frowning at what she was doing.

"Everything else in the building is old, but in here everything's new. This was built recently. I bet the drop ceiling hides an older, high ceiling, and there might be some venting or something to crawl through in the new wall."

"You're really going to go up there?" Zach asked.

"Brace the table and I will," Alice said. "It'll be just like climbing the monkey bars on the playground back in elementary."

Zach stared at her in awed amazement. "Do you even think this will work?" he asked.

She looked back at him. "It works in the movies." She jumped, caught the metal supports, and pulled herself up into the dark as though she was in gym class.

"Even if you get to the other side," called Poppy, "the door's still locked."

Zach started grinning. "No. Miss Katherine leaves the key in it. If she can get to the other side, she really can open the door. We're getting out of here."

"Ow," Alice said from above them, muffled by the tiles still in place. "I can't see the vent."

"Maybe there isn't one," Poppy said. "Come back down."

They heard a metallic clang and a sharp yelp, then more clanging. Zach hoped against hope that Miss Katherine's office was soundproof. Then the clanging stopped and there was a solid sound, like a body hitting the floor.

Poppy looked at Zach, a kind of wild hope in her eyes. He grinned at her.

Then the door opened, Alice standing on the other side and breathing heavily. "Come on," she said. "Quick."

"Okay," said Zach. "Here's the plan. We all go look for the Queen. I'll take the basement. Poppy, you retrace your steps. Alice, you take the stacks on this level. We all meet up on the side of the library—the one that's close to the street. Okay?"

"What if we don't find her?" Alice asked.

"We have to find her," Poppy said.

"Since we're split up, we're not going to know who finds what, so we just have to cover as much ground as we can and then meet up." Miss Katherine might be back soon. She could have gone out for the promised lunch, but that still didn't give them much extra time. They had to be quick. "See you guys in ten."

Poppy nodded and started toward the couches. Alice saluted and headed for the stacks.

Zach walked down the stairs to the basement. He felt a little bit guilty knowing he had a reason for deciding to look for the Queen in the basement—a reason that only sort of had to do with finding her. He wanted to read about the Kerchner guy who'd made the pottery. He wanted to know if he was really some relative of Eleanor's.

The basement was quiet, the only sound coming from the wind blowing through the window they'd left open. It was dark in the hallway, and he could see why he hadn't noticed the display: the lights in the case were off. He felt along the wall until he found the switch and flicked it.

Suddenly the cabinet sprang to bright life. The pieces inside were made of some porcelain so thin that it was practically translucent and shaped into the most fantastical forms. There were teapots corded with garlands of tiny perfect flowers; egg cups shaped with a filigree netting in the quatrefoil pattern of old church windows, all of it in shining gold; and vases with intricately shaped arms, their bodies painted with a delicate pattern of cherry blossoms. All the pieces seemed to glow from within, so thin and fine was the bone china from which they were made.

They were just like the pieces in Zach's dream of Eleanor, except that these were perfect.

And there was a plaque in the center with a black-and-white picture of a stern-looking man standing near the river. It read:

> Despite the successes of American potteries in East Liverpool at the turn of the century, they were still considered no match for their European cousins. Patriotism and ambition pushed Wilkinson-Clark China to make something unique, a new porcelain so fine that it would secure the place of their company as not just equal to, but better than any the world over. They wanted to make art.
>
> Orchid Ware was the result of a collaboration between two men: Philip

Dowling and Lukas Kerchner. Dowling was a pottery technician and a specialist in clay chemistry. He had considerable experience and was able to come up with the process that allowed Wilkinson-Clark to create a porcelain that was very thin but also possessed sufficient structural integrity for commercial production. Part of what made the porcelain so solid was the high percentage of bone ash from cattle bones that were degelatinized and then calcinated at very hot temperatures.

Kerchner was the artist. Rumored to be difficult to work with and often found shouting at underlings or accusing them of spying on him, he was also a genius, able to coax beauty from clay. His steady hand, wild imagination, and myriad influences—Art Nouveau, Moorish, Persian, and Indian, as well as the English and German pottery of his childhood—helped him make Orchid Ware objects that were wholly different and altogether finer than any porcelain produced in East Liverpool before. Kerchner became obsessive, working around the clock and refusing to allow the sale of any piece that was less than perfect.

Orchid Ware took off immediately. Highlighted at the World's Fair in Chicago, it won numerous awards and stunned the international ceramics community. Immediately there was demand among the discerning ladies of the day. Even the First Lady commissioned a piece. But despite the flood of orders, Orchid Ware turned out not to be profitable to produce. Each individual piece took too much time to complete, and many were destroyed in kilns built to fire much sturdier ceramics. Others broke during shipping. For every piece that survived, fifteen were either broken or deemed too imperfect to be salable. But despite the drain Orchid Ware was on the company's finances, Wilkinson-Clark's pride forced them to continue producing it, even at a loss.

Then tragedy struck. Lukas Kerchner's daughter went missing in the early autumn of 1895. Quickly, though, sympathy turned to terror when blood and hair were discovered in his office in the factory and on a leather apron belonging to him. It was hypothesized that he had murdered his daughter and used the method of calcinating cattle bone to dispose of her body. This was backed up by the accounts of his late wife's sister, who had been a caretaker to the daughter, and who reported Lukas Kerchner coming home in an unhinged state of mind and locking her in one of the rooms in their large Victorian home. When she escaped from the room, he and his daughter were already missing.

Lukas Kerchner denied murdering his daughter, but gave no explanation for the evidence found in his work space, nor an account of his daughter's whereabouts, saying only, "I am not her killer, but I am the one who has given her new life." Further questioning caused him to break down, screaming and weeping and insisting that his daughter "was like an angel who fell to Earth" and was "his most perfect creation." He was convicted of murder and sentenced to execution.

After his conviction, the production of Orchid Ware ceased. All told, pieces were made for less than three years, but are still avidly collected today and are very valuable. Every few years, rumors surface of fantastical pieces made by Lukas Kerchner at the height of his madness—samovars, a working porcelain clock, and even a jointed doll—although given the fragile nature of Orchid Ware, these rumors are unlikely to prove true. Still, the mystique of Orchid Ware persists and will probably persist for many years to come.

This collection is on loan from a private collector.

Zach stared at the plaque. He read through it again to be sure he understood it, his own dream echoing in his ears. If what he and Poppy had dreamed was true, if Eleanor was real, then Lukas Kerchner didn't kill his daughter. Her aunt must have caused Eleanor to fall off the roof, and Lukas—who, murderer or not, was clearly supercrazy—must have found her body and decided that the only fitting tribute was to turn her into a doll made from his precious Orchid Ware.

A shudder ran through him. It felt like electricity sparking over his skin.

Upstairs, he heard a sound like someone calling out—maybe calling a name. Miss Katherine must be in the library looking for them. Zach didn't have any more time to worry about Lukas Kerchner. He had to find the doll. He had to find Eleanor.

Quickly he walked into the first room they'd come into from the window. It was carpeted in blown paper, making the floor seem covered in fallen snow. There was no doll, though. Not on any of the filing cabinets or on the bookshelf on the far end or underneath the desks.

Crossing the hall, he went into another room, this one piled with boxes of books. He peered into each, but there was no sign of the Queen.

Then, not sure where else to look, he ducked into the girls' bathroom. He'd never been in the girls' room before, and there was something embarrassing about it. He definitely didn't want to get caught there. Looking around, though, it wasn't that different from a boys' bathroom. The tile was pink, and there were no urinals on the wall, just a row of three stalls and a single sink—but otherwise, it was identical. He walked toward the sinks and the mirror without much hope, until he noticed the metal trash can resting against one wall.

The Queen was there, lying inside the trash can, on a bed of wadded-up paper towels, her odd eyes staring up at Zach. He took a sudden, startled step back and met his own gaze in the mirror.

But even that was strange. Instead of his regular skin, he saw a face made from cracked white china with black holes where the eyes should have been. And when he opened his mouth to scream, his reflection stayed perfectly serene, lips motionless on what seemed almost like a mask.

Then he blinked and he was looking at his own face. Everything was normal, except that his heart was hammering against his chest.

He told himself that maybe Poppy had gotten up in the middle of the night and come down to use the bathroom. Maybe she'd been half-asleep and had left the Queen on a sink and the doll had fallen into the trash. It was a weird explanation, but he was going to assume that was what had happened. Otherwise, he was going to have to accept that she'd lured him to the basement so he'd read her story. Maybe later he'd be okay with thinking about that, like once he was out in the sunshine again.

He was also going to assume that he'd freaked himself out and that's why he'd thought he saw something in the mirror—something that clearly wasn't there.

Zach leaned down and carefully took the Queen out of the trash. Holding her to his chest, he started to run—out the door and up the stairs, hitting the front door of the library with his shoulder and plunging out into the cold autumn day.

ɔ CHAPTER SIXTEEN ɔ

ALICE WAS ALREADY WAITING ON THE SIDE OF THE library, squatted down and half-hidden behind a bush. She was about to say something when she spotted the Queen in his arms and jumped up.

"You did it," she said in a half whisper. "You found her!"

He nodded vigorously. "Where's Poppy?"

But just as the words came out of his mouth, Poppy rounded the corner of the building, running toward them. He caught a glimpse of pink hair behind her. "Go!" she shouted. "Go! Go!"

They pelted down the street, racing through winding roads that led to Main. After a few blocks, Zach paused, panting. When he looked back over his shoulder, he didn't see Miss Katherine anymore. He wasn't sure the librarian's bright-yellow shoes with the bows were the kind that you could run in.

"We made it," Zach said.

"You found the Queen." Poppy smiled at him. She hadn't smiled like that since before he'd lied to her about William, since before they started the quest.

He found himself grinning back. "I found something else, too. About her story. I think I know what she wanted us to find out."

"Not now," said Alice, shaking her head. "We've got to keep moving. For all we know, the librarian might be calling the cops."

"Do you still have the directions to the cemetery?" Zach asked Poppy.

Poppy nodded. "But we aren't going to make it there on foot. Unless—" Then she took off again, racing up Main Street.

They ran after her. She stopped in front of the gaming store, where a few bikes rested, some chained to a nearby pole and two leaned against a wall. She eyed them speculatively.

"You can't be serious," Zach said. "We're just going to—"

Poppy picked one up and started to walk with it

toward Alice. "You pedal," Poppy told her. "I'll get on the handlebars. And I'll tell you where to go."

Alice nodded, throwing her leg over the bike and steadying it.

"No worse than taking the boat," Poppy said, climbing up onto the front of the bike. "We'll bring them back. If we're fast enough, maybe whoever they belonged to won't even have finished their game yet."

Shaking his head, he grabbed the other unlocked bike. Shoving the Queen inside his sweatshirt, and with one arm holding the old, creepy doll in place, he mounted the seat and pedaled off after Poppy. They whizzed down the street, hair blowing behind them, his legs pumping harder and harder as they sped on.

"This way," Poppy shouted against the wind, a flimsy piece of paper blowing in one hand, the other arm extended to indicate an upcoming left turn.

He felt the same elation he had aboard the little Sunfish: the certainty that they were going to make it and the pleasure that came from solving a problem that had only minutes before seemed insurmountable. Only now, looking back, did he realize how truly crazy their middle-of-the-night plan to find Eleanor Kerchner's grave had been. But here they were, within minutes of the cemetery. They might turn out to be the kind of people who finished quests after all.

At that thought, he felt something move inside his shirt.

Zach's bike wobbled, and he nearly crashed. He skidded to a halt instead, breathing raggedly. Alice zoomed ahead, down the street.

"Stop it," he told the Queen firmly, not caring if he sounded like a lunatic. "I get that you're excited. I get that we're really close to the end. And I even get that you like to freak me out. But I don't have my bike helmet, and you're made of some superthin Orchid Ware, so if we crash, we're both going to break. Okay?"

The doll didn't move, which didn't mean anything, since the squirming might just have been his imagination. He pushed off the road and started to pedal again just as Alice and Poppy rode onto the lawn of the Spring Grove Cemetery.

He followed them, dismounting and dropping his bike beside theirs on the soft grass near the entrance, wheels still spinning. The graveyard was a tidy meadow of trimmed hedges and orderly stones. They spread out over the hill that ran up against a wooded area. A path of white gravel veered along the side, barely wide enough for a car.

"Okay," Alice said. "Now what?"

"We look for a willow tree," said Poppy. "You know, one of the ones with the long branches and the leaves that hang down."

"A *weeping* willow?" Zach put in.

Poppy nodded. "I think so, but I think regular willows have leaves that hang down too, just not as far."

"Okay," Alice said. "Depressed-looking trees. Got it. If it seems droopy and miserable at all, I'm calling you to confirm its willowy status."

Zach unzipped his sweatshirt and glanced toward Poppy. "Hey. You want to go back to carrying Eleanor?"

Poppy smirked. "How come? Does she make you nervous?"

Zach shrugged. "I just thought that you'd want her, since you brought her all this way. But if you don't—"

Poppy put out her hands. "I do, coward."

He handed over the Queen with great relief. Now when he looked at her, he couldn't help but believe she really was made from the bones of a dead girl. It made touching her shuddersome. He didn't care if Poppy teased him. He didn't want to carry the doll through the cemetery surrounded by dead people.

"Yell if you see anything," said Alice. "Like willow trees . . . or zombies."

Zach forced a laugh as they walked through the quiet graveyard, past flowerpots and wreaths, past statues to fallen soldiers and memorial benches and a large expanse of grass dotted with bronze grave markers. They passed fat oak trees, a smallish collection of pine trees, and something that Zach thought might be a locust tree, but which was definitely not a willow.

"I don't see the tree," Alice said finally. "Are you sure this is the right graveyard?"

"We're missing it somehow," said Poppy nervously. She couldn't keep still, running ahead of them and then back again. "We have to be. The grave is supposed to be *under a willow tree.*"

They kept walking, crossing the same ground, staring at the same trees.

"Maybe we should just look for the name—for Kerchner," Zach said. He wanted to tell them about the plaque in the library, but he wasn't sure how much time they had—after all, Miss Katherine had seen the maps of the cemetery.

"It's not here," Poppy said finally, her voice very small. "I really thought—after you found Eleanor back at the library—I really thought that the grave was going to be here. I thought it was going to work."

Zach flopped down on the grass in front of a large

memorial. He'd thought the same thing. "Could you be wrong about the graveyard? I mean, could there be a different one in East Liverpool?"

"Yeah," she said. "I could be wrong about that. I could be wrong about everything."

"What do you mean?" Alice asked, hopping up to sit atop a granite headstone and folding her legs under her. "Don't give up. We're so close."

Poppy remained standing, pacing back and forth on the grass. "Maybe I made it all up. All the stuff I said. I really did dream about her. But the rest . . . I don't know. It *felt* true when I said it. But I wanted it to be true so much that maybe I convinced myself it was."

For a moment they were quiet. It felt like the Earth had tilted on its axis, for Poppy to say that. She'd been the reason they'd come all this way, the reason they'd slept in the woods, sailed a boat down the Ohio River, and escaped from a library. She'd been the one who believed, no matter what. Zach had never imagined she had any doubts.

Fury rose up in him, terrible and formless. It felt like coming home and finding his figures gone all over again—as if something had been snatched away and he couldn't get it back.

Alice took a quick breath, like she was swallowing her need to scream "I knew it!" at the top of her lungs.

No magic. Just a story.

But he'd dreamed about Eleanor and he'd seen the plaque on the wall of the library. He'd felt her move and he'd seen her bones.

So maybe Poppy was just like Alice and him, doubting herself sometimes. Maybe all that meant was that she didn't know everything.

"Look, *I* think the ghost is real," Zach said.

"Maybe I just tricked you," said Poppy miserably.

It just figured that Poppy would be as stubborn about being talked *back* into believing something as she was about being talked out of believing things. "What about the guy on the bus and the donut man both saying something about there being a blond girl with us? And even the lady at the diner asked if we wanted seats for four. What about that?"

Poppy folded her arms. "The first guy was crazy. The second guy was kidding. And the diner thing was a coincidence."

"What about the camp getting trashed?" Alice asked.

"You never thought that was because of the ghost," said Poppy. "You never believed in Eleanor, Alice, so don't try to pretend."

"Did you do it?" Alice asked her. "I didn't believe it because I thought maybe it was you."

"No!" Poppy looked genuinely shocked.

"Well, then," said Alice. "Look, I didn't want to believe, but I have to admit that a lot of weird things have happened, and you have to admit it too."

Zach took a deep breath. "Remember when I said I found something back at the library? It was an exhibition of pottery—of the pottery that a Lukas Kerchner made—and there was information on his life. He supposedly *murdered his daughter*, but they *never found the body*. That can't be a coincidence. He must have been her father. And I think the secret that Eleanor wanted us to discover was that it was her aunt who killed her—the woman in the dream who chased her around the roof with a broom. She fell to her death, and her father took her body and made it into a doll because he was clearly some kind of a head case. But he didn't kill her, even though everyone thought he did. And the whole thing proves that you're right. That your dreams are real."

Poppy looked at him skeptically. "Maybe I read the story before—maybe I read about it and then forgot it, so I made up a different version of what happened."

"Oh, come on," Alice said. "That's ridiculous."

"Okay," Poppy said. "Maybe Zach is lying to make me feel better."

Zach shook his head. "I had a dream, too, that night in the woods. About Eleanor. It was . . . like yours. Alice, tell her."

"*You* had a dream?" Poppy's incredulity stung. He remembered how many times he'd spoken to her in that tone of voice since they'd started this journey and was suddenly very sorry. "How come this is the first time you're mentioning it to me? And anyway, if they *couldn't find her body*, would she even have a grave? Maybe there's nothing to find."

"Fine," Zach said, running his fingers through his hair. "What do you want me to say? We can't find the weeping willow. I don't know what to do either."

Alice slid off the stone and hugged Poppy around the waist, resting her chin against Poppy's shoulder. "It's okay. It was still an adventure, right? Our last game."

The words went through Zach like water. He took a deep breath and steeled himself. "There's something I have to tell you. Before we go back. I might as well say it now, while Poppy's already mad at me."

Poppy and Alice looked down at him, something in his tone signaling that whatever it was would be important. They watched him as if he was a snake, rearing back to strike.

"When I said that I didn't want to play anymore—" He stopped, not sure he could go on. "It wasn't true exactly. My dad threw out all my— He threw out everything. All of them. William and Tristan and Max. Everybody. So it's not so much that I don't *want* to play. I *can't*."

There was a long silence. "Why didn't you tell us?" Alice asked finally.

"I couldn't. I couldn't, because if I did, then—" He stood up, wiping his eyes. "Look, I'm sorry I didn't tell you. And I'm sorry I didn't tell you about the dream. I don't know why I didn't."

Poppy just stared at him, her eyes as hard as the Queen's.

"Okay," he said, taking a few steps back. Tears were burning in his eyes already, and he was suddenly sure there was no way they would understand. He felt stupid for telling them. He felt stupid for crying. If only he'd kept his mouth shut, everything would have been fine. "How about we all make one more sweep? We can meet back here in a couple of minutes."

"Zach," Poppy said. "Wait—"

He didn't want to hear how the quest was all his fault, how she would have never taken the Queen out of the case if it wasn't for his lie; he already knew. He staggered off before she could finish, long legs carrying him over the uneven ground. He passed rows and rows of marble stones, heading deeper into the old part of the cemetery, where the markers were chipped and weathered. There he flopped down in the grass and let himself cry in big, heaving sobs.

Saying the words out loud—saying what he'd been avoiding this whole time, that William and the rest of them were gone forever, that the game had been taken away from him, that he still wanted to play but couldn't—hurt. It ripped away the fog of numbness and even though it hurt, for the first time since he'd lost his figures, he was ready to let go.

He wasn't sure how much time had passed when he finally stopped crying. It was a beautiful day—crisp, the way early fall days can be warm but have an occasional chill wind. The sky overhead was as blue as spilled ink from a pen. Leaves shivered above him.

He leaned back and watched the clouds blow across his vision.

"Hey!" he heard Alice shout. "He's here."

"We were worried," Poppy said, standing over him and looking down. "We thought you would come back after a minute, and then we thought you would come back after ten minutes, but you didn't."

"I've been a jerk," Zach said. "I know. We've all been mad at each other, and I know a lot of it is because of what a jerk I've been."

Poppy sat down next to him. "You should have just told us."

"I know," he said. "Are you mad?"

Poppy nodded. "Of course I'm mad! But I guess I'm less mad than when I thought you didn't care about any of it."

He looked over at Alice. She was staring at one of the stones, as if maybe she didn't want to look at him. "What about you, Alice—?"

"Get up," she said suddenly. "Get up! Get up! Look!"

Poppy jumped up and hauled Zach to his feet.

Alice was pointing to a stone he'd been lying in front of on the grass. "You found it! Zach, you actually found it."

The large marble headstone bore the word KERCH-NER on it, and over that, a carving of a willow tree. They stared at it, incredulous smiles giving way to genuine grins and laughter.

It made him feel, for a moment, like maybe *no* stories were lies. Not Tinshoe Jones's stories about aliens. Not Dad's stories about things getting better or

things getting worse. Clearly, not Poppy's stories about the Queen. Maybe all stories were true ones.

Poppy knelt down, pushed aside some weeds, and traced smaller words at the base. "There are names here—it's a family plot. That's why the stone is so big. There's Lukas. And someone named Hedda—that must be Eleanor's mother. And look—a blank spot. An empty place for Eleanor."

"We did it," Alice said, her voice soft as any prayer. "The quest is complete."

"We have to give her a good funeral," said Zach. "We came all this way. We have to do it right."

Alice and Poppy nodded.

And so they decided that Zach would dig the grave, which he did mostly with his hands, but also with the assistance of several sticks and a long, flat piece of slate that was sharp enough on one end to cut through roots. It took some time, but he was able to hollow out a space big enough for the doll to rest comfortably.

Alice's job was to find flowers. She didn't want to take them from other graves, so she picked some toad lily and goldenrod and turtlehead that grew in the woods at the edge of the cemetery. She braided all the stems together to make a garland for the Queen and then made another little bouquet to leave behind once they were done.

Poppy's job was to prepare the doll for burial. She rubbed the dirt off the porcelain with spit and the cleanest edge of her T-shirt. Then she took off her hoodie and wrapped Eleanor in it, like it was a shroud.

Finally they were ready.

Poppy placed the doll in the hole in the ground and smoothed the hairs around her face. One of the doll's eyes was open, staring up at them, but the other was closed. Poppy cleared her throat.

"Eleanor," she said, "we think that you were about our age when you died and that no one really knows your true story, only that something terrible happened. We're going to keep trying to discover the truth for you. We hope you can rest easy now. You're home with your family."

"Eleanor," Zach said. The words came easily, the way they did when he was playing, but he felt entirely like himself. "You must be one determined ghost to get us to come all this way. I know we didn't always do the best job, so thanks for not quitting on us. I'm glad you chose us to be your champions."

"Eleanor," Alice said softly, stepping forward. "I only ever knew you as our Queen, so that's how I am going to talk to you. We, your loyal subjects, quested far to bring you to this place and have gathered here this day to bid you farewell on your journey. I'm glad you're finally free from your tower."

She leaned down to place the garland around the doll's neck. Pink petals fell on the Queen's dress and hair.

"The Queen is dead," she said. "Long live the Queen."

They clasped hands, and then Poppy knelt down to begin covering Eleanor with dirt. The first handfuls covered her face, leaving her fingers, her cheeks, and her forehead bare. More earth fell until she was covered completely.

"Good-bye, Eleanor," Poppy whispered as Alice set the bouquet she'd made on top of the soft, new-turned earth. A few petals fell, dusting it gold.

Zach felt the wind rise, like the wind he'd heard singing through the trees the night he'd run home from basketball practice. He felt the same chill at his neck and he shivered, but this time he didn't run. He let it pass over him, racing on and upward. And he thought he heard, very distantly, the sound of a girl laughing.

Smiling, Zach looked out at the lines of graves as they turned to walk back to the road.

Alice kept pace with him. "I keep thinking about what Poppy said, about us all changing. We are, aren't we?"

Poppy shivered in her T-shirt. "You guys are."

Zach wrapped an arm around her shoulders. "You're cold because you gave your jacket to a ghost, and you don't think anything's different about you?"

Poppy snorted, but she didn't pull away. "That's not what she means. I'm just different like *weird*. We had this adventure together, but now we're going to go back. And I'll be the same, but you guys will keep changing."

"Quests are *supposed* to change us," Zach said.

"How about real life?" asked Poppy.

Alice picked up a blade of grass and folded it in her fingers. "What's that? Seriously. This was real. This was a story that we lived. Maybe we can live other stories too."

In the distance, Zach saw two cars pull into the graveyard. He recognized Alice's aunt's silver Toyota, with his mom's beat-up green Nissan behind it. As they drew closer he saw the shadow of his father in the passenger seat.

"This was our last game," Poppy said. "This is the end of our last game."

"Oh, I don't know," said Zach. "With the Queen gone, the kingdoms are going to be in turmoil. Lots of people want her throne, all of them willing to manipulate, scheme, and battle to get it. And with William and so many other heroes dead, it's going to be a different world. A world in chaos. Maybe we can't play it the way we used to, but we could still tell each other what happens next."

"Chaos, huh?" asked Alice, a slow grin spreading over her face. "Sounds like fun."

Poppy smiled a familiar scheming smile, her eyes alight with new hope. "You want to play?" she asked.

ACKNOWLEDGMENTS

THIS BOOK HAS LIVED IN MY HEAD AND HEART FOR A long time. I hesitated writing it for years, hoping that when I did, I could do it justice. So I have a lot of people to thank for encouraging me along the way.

Thanks to Kevin Lewis, Rick Richter, and Mara Anastas, who told me their own stories of growing up and who kept asking after this project.

Thanks to everyone on Twitter, who answered many questions about middle school, passing notes folded into the shape of footballs, and many other things with aplomb.

Thanks to my workshoppers: Ellen Kusher, Delia Sherman, Josh Lewis, Gavin Grant, and Sarah Smith, for helping me see the story I was telling. And an extra thanks to Sarah Smith, who brought several excellently creepy dolls from her personal collection to stare at us while we talked.

Thanks to Kelly Link, Sarah Rees Brennan, Cassandra Clare, and Robin Wasserman, who read this book through countless times.

Thanks to Kami Garcia for all the ghostly inspiration.

Thanks to Libba Bray for making me cry.

Thanks to Steve Berman, for going on an impromptu road trip to East Liverpool to see the pottery museum and library for ourselves.

Thank you also to the Museum of Ceramics in East Liverpool. I borrowed much of the story of "Orchid Ware" from the actual story of Lotus Ware as represented by the museum.

Thanks to Eliza Wheeler for her creepifyingly beautiful illustrations.

Thanks to my agent, Barry Goldblatt, and Joe Monti for their enthusiasm for this project and also their determination that it be the best I could make it.

Thanks to my editor, Karen Wojtyla, for understanding exactly what the book was supposed to be and how to get it there. Also, thank you for cutting all the boring bits.

Thank you to everyone at Simon & Schuster and McElderry Books for being awesome.

Thanks to my husband, Theo Black, for a lot of inspiration and for patiently listening to me read the whole thing to you.

To East Liverpool, Ohio, and East Rochester, Pennsylvania, I apologize for the mangling of geography (and bus schedules) to suit my needs. I also extend an apology to the Ohio River, which has a dam I omitted from the proceedings, due to the fact that three kids on a tiny sailboat would not have been allowed through the lock.

A Reading Group Guide to

DOLL BONES

by Holly Black

About the Book

Zach, Poppy, and Alice have been friends forever. They love playing with their action figures and toys, imagining a magical world of adventure and heroism. But disaster strikes when, without warning, Zach's father throws out all his toys, declaring he's too old for them. Zach is furious, confused, and embarrassed. He decides that the only way to cope is to stop playing . . . and stop being friends with Poppy and Alice. Then one night the girls pay Zach a visit and tell him about a series of mysterious occurrences. Poppy swears that she is now being haunted by a ghost trapped in a china doll, who claims that the doll was made from the ground-up bones of a murdered girl. They must return the doll to where the girl lived and bury it. Otherwise, the ghost says, the three children will be cursed for eternity.

Vocabulary

Some terms cited in the story may be unfamiliar to you. Use reference books or electronic research sources to find out as much information as you can about the following words: *apparatus, balked, brigands, contentious, crestfallen, cryptic, daunting, exhilarating, exasperated, incredulous, lockjaw, ominously, parody, portmanteau, silhouetted, tentatively, tetanus, trepidation, vividness.*

Prereading Activity

Doll Bones is about ghosts, but it is not a "ghost story" in the classic sense. What are some of your favorite ghost stories?

Discussion Questions

1. What Zach loves about playing are "those moments where it seemed like he was accessing some other world, one that felt real as anything." What is an experience you have had, whether playing or doing something else, when you have felt the same as Zach?

2. Why is Poppy the best at playing villains?

3. Why is Zach so concerned about Poppy's brothers seeing him play with her and Alice?

4. What problem does Alice have with boys? How does Zach feel about the way Tom talks to her?

5. What is Poppy's home like? In what ways do you think it might affect who she is and how she behaves? What assumptions might you make about someone who lived in a home like hers? Why is Zach envious of Poppy's home? What does it remind him of?

6. What is the Great Queen and what is the legend the friends created about her?

7. What are Alice's complaints about her grandmother? What complaints do you have about your own parents or guardians?

8. How would you describe Zach's relationship with his father?

9. How does Zach feel about answering the questions he receives from Alice and Poppy?

10. What is the "mysterious thing" that happened to Zach over the past summer? How has Zach been feeling

since? What does he notice about how people look at him and act around him?

11. What do you think it is that makes Zach feel suddenly "overwhelmed by a wash of terror"?

12. What does Zach sometimes find annoying about Poppy?

13. How does Zach feel about his father throwing away William and his other action figures? Has a similar thing ever happened to you? What is his father's reason for doing it? Zach's father thinks of the dolls as "just plastic." What do they represent to Zach?

14. Is all the anger Zach feels reasonable? Could there be a greater thing Zach is angry about that goes unmentioned?

15. Why is Zach unable to tell Alice and Poppy about what happened? Why do you think it's easier for him to just tell them he doesn't want to play anymore? What would you do?

16. What does Zach say to Poppy that makes him feel like a jerk?

17. What promise does Poppy make about the Great Queen?

18. What does Poppy tell Zach about her dream and the Great Queen?

19. Why does Poppy want Alice and Zach to go to East Liverpool with her? What is Zach's motivation for going along? What conditions does he demand of Alice and Poppy before agreeing to go?

20. What happens to Zach's doubts about Poppy's story when he looks into the bag?

21. Zach wonders "whether growing up was learning that most stories turned out to be lies"? What do you think? Are there any stories that you were told that turned out to be lies? How did you feel when you found out they were lies?

22. What things does Tinshoe Jones do and say that would make you think he is crazy?

23. Alice says "Everyone has a story. . . . Everyone's the hero of their story." However, Poppy disagrees. She says, "There's people who do things and people who never do—who say they will someday, but they just don't." Which do you agree with? Why is Zach inclined to agree with Poppy?

24. Zach wonders if he really knows what it means to have an adventure. What do you think it means to have an adventure? What sort of things would you expect to happen on it?

25. What do the things Poppy brings with her on the quest say about her personality?

26. How did Alice, Poppy, and Zach become friends? Who would you say is the leader of the trio?

27. What does Zach dream about? What connections are there between the things he sees in his dream and the Great Queen?

28. Who or what do you think is responsible for trashing their campsite?

29. Why does Zach desperately want ghosts to be real?

30. Zach says he would want to be a ghost if he were murdered so he could haunt his killer. Under what circumstances would you want to be a ghost?

31. Why doesn't Zach want to talk about the dream he had?

32. Why does adventuring turn out to be boring for Zach?

33. Why is Poppy so upset about Alice and Zach keeping things from her?

34. Why does Alice throw the Great Queen in the water? What does Poppy accuse her of?

35. How does Alice react to Poppy revealing her secret to Zach? Has Zach been a bad friend to Alice and Poppy?

36. Why do you think Zach decides to tell Alice about his dream?

37. Why is Alice so desperate for there not to be a real ghost?

38. What do you think Poppy means when she says "growing up . . . seems like *dying*"?

39. What makes Zach realize he wants the quest to be completed the way Poppy imagined?

40. What does Zach's father say to him that drains him of his anger?

41. What does Zach learn about Eleanor Kerchner in the library? How does what he reads relate to the dreams he and Poppy had about Eleanor?

42. What makes Zach finally tell Alice and Poppy the truth about what his father did? Do you think they would have ever undertaken this quest if he had told them the truth from the beginning?

43. When the friends lay the Great Queen to rest in the cemetery, what does each character symbolically lay to rest?

44. Zach says, "Quests are *supposed* to change us." In

what ways do the three characters change in the course of the story?

45. Zach says that with William and their heroes dead, their game will be a "world in chaos." How does adolescence represent a world in chaos?

Postreading Activities

1. Poppy calls the journey she, Zach, and Alice take a quest. A quest is a journey in the course of which one advances spiritually and mentally, as well as physically travelling miles. The quester leaves the familiar for the unknown and is often accompanied by companions. The nature of the goal may not be clear at first and may only become fully apparent at the end of the quest. In many traditional quest stories, the supernatural plays a role. Discuss how *Doll Bones* fits the definition of a quest story.

2. What do you know about superstitions? Using print and electronic resources, research superstitions and discuss the strangest ones you find.

3. Do you have a favorite doll or action figure? How did you come to have it, and how do you play with it?

4. There's a vivid description of Poppy's bedroom in the beginning of the novel. Write a detailed description of your own bedroom or of a room in your home.

5. Identify three conflicts in the story and explain how they are resolved.

6. Illustrate a favorite incident or scene from the novel.

7. Retell a favorite episode from the novel in your own words.

About the Author

Holly Black is the author of bestselling contemporary fantasy books for kids and teens. Some of her titles include The Spiderwick Chronicles (with Tony DiTerlizzi), the Modern Faerie Tale series, The Good Neighbors graphic novel trilogy (with Ted Naifeh), the Curse Workers series, *Doll Bones*, and *The Coldest Girl in Coldtown*. She has been a finalist for a Mythopoeic Award, a finalist for an Eisner Award, and is the recipient of both the Andre Norton Award and the Newbery Honor. She currently lives in New England with her husband and son in a house with a secret door. Visit her at BlackHolly.com.

This guide was written by Edward T. Sullivan, a librarian and writer.

Masks that transform the wearer.
A flute that separates a girl and her shadow.

What fateful magic lies hidden
in the heart of Zombay?

Don't miss *Goblin Secrets*, a National Book Award Winner,
and its companion, *Ghoulish Song*, by William Alexander.

★"Gripping and tantalizing."—*Kirkus Reviews*, starred review

"It was hard to stop reading *Goblin Secrets*, and I didn't want the book to end!
The author's imagination is both huge and original. More, please, Will Alexander!"
—Ursula K. Le Guin, author of the Earthsea Cycle

"Funny, smart, and gorgeously written. When I grow up, I want to be Will."
—Jane Yolen, author of *The Devil's Arithmetic*

If you are twelve, you have it:
the Ability to enter people's minds.

It's your choice whether you use it
for good . . . or for evil.

A Pokanoket boy. A young English settler.
Their unusual friendship will
change their lives forever.

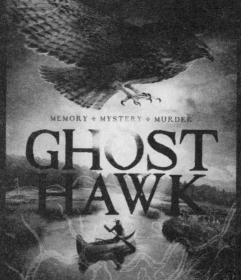

MEMORY ✦ MYSTERY ✦ MURDER

GHOST HAWK

SUSAN COOPER
NEWBERY AWARD-WINNING AUTHOR OF *THE DARK IS RISING*

★"Cooper has written a richly plotted, lyrical, and near-epic novel. . . . This is simply an
unforgettable reading experience."—*Booklist*, starred review

★"Well-researched and elegant historical fantasy."—*Publishers Weekly*, starred review

"[A] sensitive portrayal of an unusual friendship."—*Kirkus Reviews*

"I was swept up in the story, shocked, moved, and enthralled—and completely convinced
by the historical background. I haven't read anything better for a long time."
—Philip Pullman, author of *The Golden Compass*

"Beautifully written, vivid with its manifest love for the land, *Ghost Hawk* is a story of
suffering and survival, both tragic and heroic."—Karen Cushman, author of the Newbery
Medal winner *The Midwife's Apprentice*

"Susan Cooper has asked the ghosts of our shared history to sing. And when she asks, they
always do."—*William Alexander*, author of the National Book Award winner *Goblin Secrets*

PRINT AND EBOOK EDITIONS AVAILABLE
From Margaret K. McElderry Books | KIDS.SimonandSchuster.com